You have been searching for us without knowing it, following oblique references in crudely xeroxed marginal "samisdat" publications, crackpot mystical pamphlets, mail order courses ... a paper trail and a coded series of rumors spread at street level ... and the propagation of certain acts of insurrection against the *Planetary Work Machine* and the *Consensus Reality* ... or perhaps through various obscure mimeographed technical papers on the edges of "chaos science" ... through pirate computer networks ... or even through pure synchronicity and the pursuit of dreams.

In any case we know something about you, your interests, deeds and desires, works and days ... and we know your address.

Otherwise...you would not be reading this brochure...

Ong's Hat
The Beginning

Joseph Matheny
with Peter Moon

SkyBooks
Westbury, New York

*INCUNABULA : A Catalog of Rare Books, Manuscripts &
Curiosa Conspiracy Theory, Frontier Science & Alternative
Worlds* and *ONG'S HAT:GATEWAY TO THE DIMENSIONS!
A full color brochure for the Institute of Chaos Studies and
the Moorish Science Ashram in Ong's Hat, New Jersey*,
authors unknown. Used here as reference material.

Cover art and illustrations on pages 115,125, 167 by Denny
Unger as commisioned by Joseph Matheny

Illustrations on pages 165, 177 by Jon Bright as commisioned
by Joseph Matheny

Graphic novel illustrations on pages 153-1164 by Tony Talbert
as commisioned and written by Joseph Matheny

Photos on pages 148, 149, incidental art and layout by Joseph
Matheny

Library of Congress Cataloging-in-Publication Data
Joseph Matheny, 1961-
Peter Moon 1953 -
Ong's Hat: The Beginning
ISBN 0-9678162-2-X.CIP 99-0911110
Library of Congress Control Number: 2002107576

Dedications and Acknowledgments

To those who without this would not have been possible. Rob Brezsny, D.W. Cooper, Denny Unger and Darkplanet, Jonathan Latt, Rupert and Abel, Peter Moon, Nick Herbert, Elizabeth and Paddy, Nina Graboi, Dan Brandenburg and the Fringewire Network, Shanda, humdog, Jay and the memories of Avalon, Christopher and John Warnock, V00P (for all the Hotmail info), Marijana, Stephanie, Karen, Curt, Ian, Matt (thanks for all the Yahoo info), Sarah "of Swanlake", Hunter (for the laughs kiddo!), Emory (you aren't all bad), Ralph Abraham, RD @ the Princeton Egg Project, Jaron Lanier, Millbrook East and West, Antero Ali, The Professor, Big T, Pete, Chandra, Jay Kinney, Adobe Internet Products Division (GO TEAM!), Neal, the strange group in New Orleans that has no name but knows mine, Ray and Bob Flanolanger, Phil and Scott, the girls at Coffeetopia, Julie, my Grandfather, Philip K. Dick, John Nash, Gretchen Giles, deoxy.org, surfingtheapocalypse.com, disinfo.com, all the various BBSs, Gopher sites, FTP sites and websites that have come and gone over the years, the Xerox underground of the 80s and early 90s, and various colorful street people who's names I never knew.

The author's profits from this book are being donated to the Santa Cruz Homeless Garden Project in memory of the Formless Ocean Group.

Donations may be sent to:
Santa Cruz Homeless Garden Project
P.O. Box 617
Santa Cruz, CA 95061
(831) 426-3609
http://www.infopoint.com/sc/orgs/garden/

Table of Contents

Forward

If you have picked up this book and gotten this far, it is assumed that you are about to read one of the most obscure and intriguing conspiracies ever concocted by consciousness. Well, consciousness sort of works like a conspiracy. There are all sorts of principles in creation and existence yet we are only required to know and experience a small part in order to survive in our limited human existence. The original e-book format of this book was entitled *The Incunabula Papers*, but did not include everything herein. It sold well over a million copies, and one of the reasons it sold so well was that the basic premise of the conspiracy was based upon sound scientific thinking regarding the quantum principles of existence. It is also great fun. Although it has attracted many scientific and occult minds, Joseph Matheny, the man primarily responsible for the proliferation of *The Incunabula Papers* e-book, informs me that most people do not "get it." Joe has become something of a cult figure and has been pursued so strongly at times that he keeps his personal phone very private. People have spent countless hours researching the many offshoots presented here and some have come up with very interesting contributions. Nevertheless, most people still do not "get it." As I have been told that I "get it," I will try to enhance your perspective and appreciation of the material herein by approaching the subject with a narrative that contains two very distinct threads.

The first thread of my narrative concerns the subject of information. As you might imagine, I am often approached by people who have various stories to tell. More often than not, the stories require a lot of leg work in terms of rewriting and retelling. Even if they have merit, I am usually not interested because the type of research I do and am known for is highly specialized. For example, if someone calls me in emergency mode and claims that the leading bronco buster from Texas has lassoed a real live alien and that I had better get down their quick, I am not too moved. Then they say that the cowboy has tied the alien's feet to his hands and is parading him only to a select crowd, and that I am personally invited and can be the first to report on it. I will leave that to certain media hucksters. The problem with many stories of this type is that they do not do anything besides shock an already stultified audience into a titillation where they can say, "Look, see!" This is what much of the UFO and paranormal phenomena circuit has turned into. "Made ya look! Made ya look!"

One of the reasons for this is that there is a glut of information and almost everything has a certain monotone of relative unimportance. Only the shock of terrorism or a spectacular murder investigation seems to ride above the wave of dull and bored media hosts. Observing UFO phenomena and related information has become as complicated as ever. The military now seems to have spacecraft as sophisticated as anything sci-fi authors could have imagined in the 1950's. If they do not, you would have to assume that they must be programmed drones at the highest level. Assimilating, processing, and evaluating information has become an intimidating task in what can now be termed the dawn of the Information Age. The media puts out phoney stories on television and the conspiracy theorists counter them. Both outlets leave a lot to be desired as neither seem to focus on the relevant truths. Even when conspiracy theorists, patriots, or militia people are completely right on a particular issue, their banner of truth just seems to flap in the wind, easily ignored by the media authorities. Information has become the new commodity in the environment. It is also power. The media can completely influence an issue by the nature of the information they propagate. Information has even become somewhat senior to nature with the developments in genetics whereby information can be programmed into nature. The media has jumped on the phrase "the Information Superhighway" which basically refers to all of the information that can be accessed on the internet. While the internet is certainly an amazing superhighway of information, the term Information Superhighway refers to much more than that.

Nature and all of existence include many unseen processes as well as the readily observable ones. The Information Superhighway also includes many unseen factors. Computer analysts and users are always running into quirks and other things they do not fully understand. The industry has their own words for such things. Today, we now have internet police who do far more than just police ordinary crime and the like. They counter potential threats to the established moral climate which, of course, includes certain conspiracy authors. It is like the old black and white cars of the California Highway Patrol (C.H.P.) pulling over anyone who looks suspicious. Control of information has become a serious occupation. There is a desire to suppress certain information, particularly the type of information that is in this book and any other information that would expand your consciousness. It is refreshing however to report that there is at least one vehicle who has eluded the C.H.P. It is a souped-up hearse that is insulated from bullets and can out maneuver those old black and whites. The man who drives the hearse also built the black and whites, or at least helped in their design. That is why the hearse, a bigger and more durable vehicle, can out maneuver the police. In fact, they leave him alone for the most part. But, why does he drive a hearse?

Well, that analogy refers to the fact that he not only negotiates the Information Superhighway, but that he drives off of the road and explores the surrounding area as he picks up all the discarded information and puts it in the back of the hearse. After all, there are not human bodies in there, but there is "dead information" so to speak. You might call him the Grim Reaper of dead information, information which has been relegated to the scrap heap of ordinary existence.

While the term "occult" more properly means "hidden" (with reference to knowledge or information), I have also seen it defined as "rejected knowledge." In other words, information that has been rejected because it is either not understood or of no known use. Nevertheless, it is still information. The man in the hearse collects all of this information which can range from ordinary binary digits to huge hard drives and main frames. He studies it and assimilates it into a computer that he has constructed in the back of the hearse. After all, he is a computer expert. But, a good share of the information in the machine is quite different from that which you would find on the ordinary Information Superhighway of Earth in the 21st Century. People do not understand it and, after all, not too many people want to look too closely at a hearse, let alone what might be in the back of it!

We'll get back into what exactly is in the back of the hearse in just a bit, but now I am going to introduce you to the second thread in my narrative: the Knights Templar, a secret order of holy knights who arose to prominence during the Crusades and became the preeminent power during that time period. They are juxtaposed in a very relevant and interesting way to Ong's Hat when we consider their role in the millennium prior to the Information Age. According to the ancient science of astrology and the measurement of the Precession of the Equinox, we are emerging from the darkest yuga (period of 26,000 years) of our history. The end of this dark Yuga reached it's peak during the last two thousand years when our planet was tilted the maximum amount away from the center of light in the middle of our galaxy. This was known as the Age of Pisces. Our new age is Aquarius, the Water Bearer (In occultism, water refers to emotions; so maybe, just maybe, this new era will enable you to reconnect with all those emotional ties of the past, the loves and friendships of antiquity.) which corresponds to the Information Age. The computer revolution is a reassembly of information new and old. Things are just getting started, but it will take a while. As a general subject, information resourcing has been on a serious decline during the last yuga, ultimately climaxing in the Age of Pisces when the Library of Alexandria was burned. After this point, all schools of wisdom went completely underground.

One of these schools of wisdom was the Knights Templar who originally received their wisdom in ancient initiatic ceremonies from the Ismaili sect of Islam, a very misunderstood group, the descendants of which are arguably raising a bit of havoc in the Mideast as I write this. The Ismailis were the keepers of wisdom for their day, but they were a minority sect as far as the rest of Islam was concerned. They evolved into the Assassins and protected their turf like demons from hell. Extreme conditions require extreme measures. I do not think they were very fond of the Muslims who sacked the Library of Alexandria. Maybe you can better understand why their descendants are so passionate about their causes. Losing the library at Pharos was akin to the hard disk of planet Earth suffering a crash. The Ismailis witnessed the Templars in the Holy Land and saw in them kindred spirits who both had a common enemy: the orthodox Caliph of Islam. The genetic lines of the Templars and Ismailis eventually intertwined through common marriages, but Muslim orthodoxy was never overtly challenged and overcome to any significant extent, although there was a renaissance and a brief spurt of culture in Andalusia. The trend during the Age of Pisces was not to stand and fight for your turf but to go underground. This was aptly portrayed in the Grail Romances where a Saracen (popular term for a Muslim during the Middle Ages which originally referred to a Moorish Muslim from Sargasso, Spain) was always featured as the standard bearer of wisdom who carried the torch of liberty.

As the collective consciousness descended into the Age of Pisces, the Templars carried what remaining embers and flames were left of the original torch that used to blaze brightly from the lighthouse of Pharos. If you compare the Templars to computer operators, they were operating a hard disk that was barely alive. There were a lot of bad blocks and clusters, but somehow, just enough of the system was operating that it could keep things going. It was as if the Earth's Information Superhighway had been running on an Uninterruptable Power Supply only. The Templars represented the power supply. For those of you who have ever tried to repair a hard drive on an old personal computer that had an antiquated operating system, you know that you can end up employing some very unusual solutions just to keep things running. Somehow, after all the repair programs have been utilized and failed, you wrap a cable in aluminum foil or do something else unusual and everything seems to work — for a while. You do not understand exactly how you got it working or why it is working. You just know that you have a certain affinity or "psychic read" on the computer and you are proud of yourself for getting it to work even though you know you need a new one. This is what happened to the Templars. During this era of darkness, they were running the computer system of the planet through the Crystal Skull of Golgotha (the word Golgotha means "skull" or "place of the skull"). Public documents revealed many of the Templars confessed under torture to worshipping a mysterious head. Historical writers have never figured anything out beyond this as they generally have limited experience and only believe things if they see that someone else wrote it. A lot of the communications the Templars made were fuzzy and some were degenerate and, in some cases, the skull was replaced by lower harmonic representations. They accepted Baphomet as a "coprocessor" because they had nothing better. Max Headrom or television anchormen could have also filled in just as well but they were completely unavailable. In all seriousness however, the Templars had plugged into the information grid of the planet. When the Templars accessed Baphomet, which can mean "Father of All Wisdom," they were accessing the skeletal architecture of the Earth's computer itself. Baphomet, in part, also represents the lower aspects of incarnating into the Earth plane. So much mystery has been built up around the Templars, but they were simply hanging on desperately in an aberrant dramatization of sexual rites which could be likened to a dying man spontaneously ejaculating on a purely biological basis as a last ditch effort to survive or procreate in order to prevent death. After a brief heyday during the Crusades, the Templars became a dying breed. The Grand Master, Jacque DeMolay, was literally roasted over a fire on Friday, October 13, 1314. Finally, the rejected bits of knowledge of the Templars ended up on the shoulder of the Information Super Highway where it was picked up by our friend in the hearse who integrated it into his super computer in the rear. That computer has a lot of other interesting things in it, too, but we will address that later.

I have chosen the Templars in this analogy for a very good reason. The heritage passed on to them from the Ismailis or Assassins indoctrinated them as torch bearers of the flame of liberty in the West. As you read *Ong's Hat: The Beginning* you will run across references to obscure Islamic connections and to the Moorish Orthodox Church, a religious body who seek to carry on this tradition today. They are all part of the same thread no matter how good or bad the various individuals involved in the respective orders may or may not be. This analogy will give you some context and the ancient traditions which the legend of Ong's Hat very much embodies.

The relationship between the Ismailis and the Templars was like one computer language being transferred into another, but where the transference took place is even more important in our analogy. The Templars received their initiation from the Assassins in a location which could be likened to a tape backup system for a computer: beneath the Dome of the Rock which had once been part of the Temple of

14

Solomon. The Templars occupied the stables underneath which lead yet deeper into honeycombed caves that are better suited for a ride at Disney World. These pathways were also the means of retreat for certain archives of antiquity and that is why I compared them to a tape backup. The Temple of Solomon can be likened to the central processing unit or even the kernel of the computer itself. It's architecture allowed for the life of electricity to come in and activate the entire system. Housing the Ark of the Covenant, the Temple of Solomon represents the highest aspirations of Abramic man in the post Babylonian Era. It was the conduit to the original powers of Creation. The Jews hope to reaffirm their relationship with the Creator by having the Temple of Solomon rebuilt. Unfortunately for them, certain Islamic real estate is in the way. Currently, the Dome of the Rock, where Abraham tried to sacrifice his son Isaac, is a mosque which stands on that ground and belongs to the Muslims. It is the third most holy site in Islam. According to common history, it was originally passed on to the Muslims by insistent Jews who no longer wanted it. Caliph Omar, who really did not want to be bothered with it, interrupted his busy plans to receive it.

Fundamentalist Christians are very eager for the Temple to be rebuilt because they believe the messiah will return. The Jews believe he will come for the first time. For Christians and Jews, this is not much of a disagreement for they will both recognize the messiah. Their dispute is really just a question of whether or not he is appearing in the World Series for the first time. Whether or not he has appeared or will appear, Ariel Sharon has already thrown out the first pitch. According to undernourished media reports, the suicide bombings of 2001-2002 did not actually begin until Ariel Sharon visited the Dome of the Rock and began to stake out his territory with over a thousand bodyguards. According to reports, to put it politely, he did this in a very territorial manner. This shook the Arabs to their very core because it represents the dismantling of their holy site, the locale (same as the Temple of Solomon) where the Prophet ascended to heaven on a horse.

As I write this in the Spring of 2002, Israel is at war with Yasser Arafat and the Palestinians. Obsessed and ignorant media pundits like to refer to the suicide bombers as crazed mind control victims who believe they will be taken to heaven where they will be serviced by seventy-two virgins. "How wacky can that be?" they say to their stupefied television audiences.

Thus far, I have witnessed at least two major flaws with regard to the American media's virulent approach to how they view suicide bombers. Most are emotionally incapable of fully acknowledging the Palestinian viewpoint. They are repelled by suicide bombings and so am I, but these guys suffer an intellectual shut down. Just because it is reprehensible and extremely hurtful does not mean that you should stop looking for further truth and information. It is understandable that most Americans cannot relate to Arab culture, but the major flaw is that they fail to mention or recognize that Jews are more famous than almost anyone else for committing suicide. Remember the story of Masada, the mountain fortress that was inaccessible and was the last defense of the Jewish culture? The Jewish zealots committed suicide in mass, even killing their own women and children, rather than give in to the Roman occupation. The Romans were not trying to kill the Jews; they were just trying to make them a subject people. This was just after the Romans had sacked the Holy City and destroyed the Temple of Solomon. The Jewish suicide was even homicidal in the case of the children who did not take their own lives. This was the most virulent form of protest one can imagine. Of course, you can say that suicide does not count as a valid of form of protest but that is judgmental. Protest is protest and people will protest anyway they want. How they protest is directly proportional to the degree of oppression. I would say that having your Holy Temple ransacked along with your holy relics is a pretty oppressive experience. Although the Jews of Masada did commit homicide on their own kind, they did not wire explosives to themselves in order to kill the enemy. They did not have such means, but if they did, it would have been a logical approach to defending themselves under such extreme oppression. It could not have been much worse than the fate they ultimately inflicted upon themselves.

The second major flaw concerning the media and their approach to the suicide bombers is when they laugh or ridicule the idea of seventy-two virgins. I do not expect them to be very conversant with esoteric information so their ignorance is somewhat excusable, but the flaw in their comprehension is extremely large.

Seventy-two is a sacred number and refers to different things, but the most obvious occult reference is to the seventy-two Keys of Solomon. These were the means and methods he use to control the Jinn and manifest anything his heart desired. These seventy-two aethyrs were frequencies that enlisted the elementals of earth, air, water and fire. It is not only a rather involved study in itself, it is the ultimate study when it comes to the riddle of existence. The point here is that the idea of seventy-two virgins has a religious and esoteric depth that is far beyond the comprehension of media pundits who do not even know what they are speaking of. Solomon was known as Sulaiyman to the Arabs and was respected immensely for his occult powers. The connection between the rebuilding of the Temple by the Jews and the magical correspondences and heritage of Solomon himself should not be overlooked. The Templars and the Assassins are characterized with much intrigue and mystery, but too few have realized that there are considerably more fireworks and wonder to be experienced when studying Solomon.

David was the first real King of Israel and his son Solomon, for all practical purposes, was the last. Actually, Solomon's son (of the tribe of Judah) was a terrible and oppressive ruler who inspired the rest of the tribes to disperse. We have a separation of a united people, not unlike the disunity that followed the destruction of the Tower of Babylon. The Jews are well aware that their kingdom has never been the same since Solomon's death.

Solomon has different etymologies, of which the most popular occult one is "mountain of the sun." The Japanese like this one because it is like their sacred mountain, Mount Fujiyama. It also means "source of the Black Sun." Perhaps the most scholarly one, and my current favorite, is "peace of On" where "Solom" derives from *shalom* (Hebrew for "peace") and *On*, the biblical name for Heliopolis (the Egyptian "City of the Sun" which was completely dedicated to the worship of Ra). *Shalom* and *On* together mean "peace of On."

"On" is certainly suggestive of the word "Ong" as in Ong's Hat, but there is also another key meaning to On. Most of the general public and casual students of magic would not know it, but On refers to the greatest work of all magick. It is a combination of at least two rites: Babalon and Abrahadabra. Babalon represents the female polarity while Abrahadabra represents the male. This is too involved to go into here, but On in this sense represents the most cosmic union imaginable between the two polarities of male/female, yin/yang, etc. In a somewhat lower manifestation, On represents the incarnation of a magical child or moon child, the most notable of which (according to magical tradition) would be the virgin birth of the Christ. Some of the other experiments are not always deemed to be as successful at that particular one. *On* also appears in the word *aeon* which means "space of time," particularly a long space of time but, more properly, it derives from *ai-On* where *ai* means forever and *on* refers to time. In this sense, it refers to the eternity of *On*. The word *ontology*, which features the syllable "on," means study of the nature of being. In Greek, *on* is a participle for the word "be." In summary, we have the word *On* representing the full spectrum of being forever in the space of time which, of course, includes the process of polarity. There are other correspondences in the dictionary. The magical components are far too deep and involved to present here.

In the case of Solomon representing "the peace of On," we get the idea that this king achieved a reconciliation with the primal cosmic forces that dictate the universe. In computer lingo, you might say he had access to the source code and the programmers who could make things work for him.

Besides the above loose relationship of *On* to *Ong*, there is an excellent case to be made for On being identical to "Ong" as in "Ong's Hat" and references can be found in the magical writings of H.P. Lovecraft, a man whose work was known to be inspired or connected to legends that came out of the New Jersey Pine Barrens, the locale in New Jersey where Ong's Hat is located. By synchronicity, I ran across a note from Clark Ashton Smith to Lovecraft which displayed sigils that referred to the "lion-headed Ong." I eventually found the short story by Smith which talks about the Lion Headed Ong, the Magicians of Ong, and the Inquisitors of Ong. They are not very nice creatures by this account and it is a rather morbid tale set in a place that might best be described as a suburb of hell. The point is that the lion has always been placed with the sun (On) in astrology. Stewart Swerdlow has identified the lion frequency as being that which emanates from the throne of the Creator, a most powerful frequency. George Hunt Williamson has identified the same in his book "Secret Places of the Lion." "Lion," which contains the letters *o* and *n* also is symbolic of "gate" as in "Babalon" (which has also been interpreted as "baby lion" or "gate.") That is why lions are traditionally positioned around doorways, particularly in the Orient. Leo the Lion is the most exalted sign of the zodiac and was thus depicted as the ruler of all beasts. In this sense "Ong" is positioned with the ruling aspects of our consciousness.

If the above does not satisfy you, I refer you to page sixty-four of Kenneth Grant's *Cults of the Shadow* which reveals that *On* in Egypt referred to the sun but as the name was perpetuated in the Vedic religion, it became *Ong* or *Om*, the primal vibration of the creative spirit. Grant is very astute to note in his work, contrary to most popular assumptions, that the wisdom of tantra or magick migrated from Africa to other parts of the world. The word *Africa* itself derives from *afrit* or ifrit. Those of you who have studied the Arabian Nights will recognize the word *ifrit* as another name for a genie. The words *jinn* or *genie* derive from *genius* which means "spirit." When we consider that the word *virgin* derives from *vir* and *gin*, we understand that *virgin* denotes not only a "pure" or "true" (*vir* can mean either) spirit, but suggests an integral relationship between truth and purity and the jinn itself. In this manner, the jinn were the intermediary between mankind and the seventy-two virgins of lore. Actually, there was a hierarchal structure in some methodologies where the jinn ruled over the genies. By definition, a virgin was one who was untouched by man or the jinn. But, the true spirits were the real power in the Solomon equation. Once he had bottled the jinn, he could perform his magick by accessing the virgin energies. In this respect, those who have studied tantra might better recognize the seventy-two virgins as the Dakini or Sky Dancers as they are more commonly known.

While I will personally be expounding on the keys of Africa in a future book, it is sufficient for now to say that King Solomon's historical life was certainly a testament to him utilizing the goddess or pagan energy. In modern terms, pagan refers to any system of religion that is not of Abraham. Christianity, Judaism, and Islam all trace back to Abraham. Solomon would marry the daughters of others kings to expand his empire and avoid war. He fathered more children than we will ever know, but he certainly put his trace on humanity in a way that perhaps no other man ever has. Many names derive from Solomon. The Irish name Sullivan derived from the pronunciation of "Sulaiyman."

The stories of Solomon being punished by God are a patriarchal overtone that was written by the victors of history. The same thing happened in the stories of Babylon, Sodom and Gomorrah. Degenerate disregard for the truth and defiling of the virgin energy of the Dakini led to an abolition of any form of matriarchal culture. Solomon was just the leading representative of the last major cultural expounding of the goddess. Even so, it should be said that his culture was only a degrade of earlier such cultures because it was filled with slavery and repression. But, that was not really the point. He had power and could interface with the elementals and perform miraculous tasks. In essence, the legend and history of King Solomon represents the last hurrah of the goddess/pagan culture as it is usurped by David's God which was never actually referred to by the name "Jehovah" until recent times.

In summary, the Temple of Solomon represents a way station between the heavenly or aethyric forces and the elements of the Earth plane. It was sort of a high action zone. But, none of this means that rebuilding the Temple of Solomon in current times will bring about a similar situation. In occult tradition, constructing a temple always involves a sacrifice, almost always human. In the Temple of Solomon, the builder, who is called Hiram Abiff but was really Adonai or Adonis, was murdered and served as the sacrifice for Solomon's Temple. He has been remembered ever since in Masonic rituals. The current drama being acted out in Palestine right now might just rival the wholesale human sacrifices of the Aztecs by the time it is over. The sad irony of these efforts is that if a messiah came, she or he would not likely be recognized. If it were a man, the only valid messiah would bring about a balance of polarity and this would not be too easily recognized or accepted by the extremely patriarchal faiths of Abraham. I do not need to tell you how they would react if it were a woman, especially if her name was Gaia. Then again, maybe she is already here if you just listen to her heart beat.

All in all, the twists and turns in the Mideast makes for great television from a purely spectator's point of view and should considerably boost the news ratings. It is even more interesting when you understand the esoteric and religious components. Nevertheless, there are more important and even more interesting dramas being acted out. They are just not transmitted over the airwaves.

Although the wisdom schools of the Templars and Ismailis have suffered great attrition, their rejected information, along with the lost information of the Temple of Solomon, has been scooped up by our friend with the hearse. The pages of this book reflect that although the information is at times obtuse. You have to expect that with rejected information. It is not always easy to process and figure out. Sometimes it takes a computer expert. This is where the character in the hearse fits in.

I have used the analogy of the hearse driver to give you a very realistic interpretation of the life of Joseph Matheny as the primary author/compiler of this book. Joe has had a bizarre and colorful life that ranges from the mundane world of business and ordinary living to exotic pursuits many of you would not believe. Of primary interest to this narrative was his witnessing of and participation in the Silicon Valley revolution that ushered in the Information Age. A computer genius, to put it mildly, Joe was among the first characters to fully understand and utilize the internet. This was back in the 1980's, and he has followed and kept up to date with it ever since. With a high aptitude for computing, he did this for fun and interest, not because he was seeking a fortune. It was one of many talents that he enjoyed. Moving to Santa Cruz, California, he also found himself right in the middle of major counterculturer evolutionaries which included Robert Anton Wilson, Timothy Leary, Nick Herbert, and a host of many others too long to mention. Amidst many adventures, he soon found himself in deep trouble when a collective body of geniuses conspired to ruin him publicly and financially. Most of them were from NASA and ILM (George Lucas' Industrial Light

21

and Magic) and were deeply involved in dark occult orders. At least part of this story is scheduled to appear in an upcoming book by *Newsweek*. As the Internet began to grow, Joe's abilities and services were in demand and were eventually parlayed into the common software product which you know as Adobe Acrobat. He literally engineered that product into existence. After leaving Adobe in 1998, he pioneered another popular technology, namely the video format known as DVD. But, as I said earlier, to call him a computer genius is to put it mildly. Joe is familiar and conversant with every aspect of computer technology and capability that you can imagine. This ranges from holography to artificial intelligence. Leaving the DVD industry proper, he formed his own company and made his personal fortune during the Silicon Valley boom. This capped off a personal career that included forays into: organic chemistry, large-scale publishing, telephony, pharmaceutical, aerospace, robotics, television, radio, music, film production, and polymer/phenolic material fabrication. He is now officially retired although he is just about forty years old at this writing.

I met Joe through my own interest in Ong's Hat. You will discover how I first encountered Ong's Hat as you read this book. Although I did not then have time to pursue the subject on the internet, I put a colleague on the project. After about a years worth of correspondence with Joe, I was introduced. Much to my own interest and surprise, Joe had not lassoed an alien and branded them with WingMaker symbols or the like. In fact, I immediately found he had some answers to some of the investigations I had pursued as accounted for in the book *Montauk Revisited: Adventures in Synchronicity*. These concerned magical occult orders and the Aleister Crowley connection. I had no anticipation or expectation that he could help me in such matters. This was not the purpose of our initial contact. We were actually just getting acquainted and were going to see if he could help me with some computer matters. This soon turned into a major occult gold mine, but that is not really the subject of this narrative. This is just a short background to give context, but the occult connections will be exposed and expounded upon in a subsequent book.

Joe does not drive a hearse in real life. But if he did, you would see nude surfer girls waving at you from the rear. He has a lot of fun. The computer in the back of the hearse is another matter. He also works long hours and enjoys solitude. His position in Silicon Valley enabled him to access the fastest and most highly sophisticated computer networks in the world. As he did his regular workaday job, he piggybacked his avant garde interests and experiments into a device called the Metamachine©.

That is the inspiration for the computer system on the cover of this book. This was done by picking up the rejected data from the shoulder of the Information Superhighway and integrating it with state-of-the-art computing. The end result? That remains to be determined, but one of the most immediate results was an e-book entitled "The Incunabula Papers" which included some of the information in this book, but not all. The e-book was a multilevel document but, at least in part, it was presented in such a way as to appeal to the computer game crowd. Joe grew up with this generation and realized that many of these kids/people will never likely be exposed to much information that is consciousness expanding. Therefore, he loaded it with lots of graphics and bells and whistles. The e-book is loaded with hidden synchronistic messages if you just happen to click at the right space at the right time. It is completely random and determined by synchronicity.

What was so special about the e-book was that it was the first of its kind. Most e-books were just words by Stephen King or another very popular author. With all its graphics and polish, *The Incunabula Papers* was a leader in the industry and there was nothing else to compare it too. Using it as a demo, it was hungrily and readily gobbled up by those in e-commerce who used it as a guiding light and example for others to follow. The fact that the data was highly esoteric in nature was missed by many who encountered it in the ordinary world of e-commerce. It was a leading seller on MightyWords, a revolutionary e-book distributor which was eventually bought up by Barnes and Noble and literally put out of business. Still, between Mighty Words and downloads from his own website, well over a million copies of the e-book *The Incunabula Papers* were distributed. Joe's profits from this enterprise were donated to the Homeless Garden Project in Santa

Cruz, California. The royalties from the book you are reading will be donated to the same cause.

While all of the above may or may not be impressive to you, there has been more than a little problem concerning all of this. Whenever Joe turns on the machine in the back of the hearse, the Metamachine©, it creates more than a bit of chaos. It is like a corpse in the back rising up and creating havoc when one hopes that it might just rest in peace. It has become a burden and is something he would like to release himself from permanently; however, life is not always so easily lived. Dr. Frankenstein had to deal with his monster and Joe has to deal with his creation. The Metamachine© is not a toy. It manifested through Joe by reason of various forces in conjunction with his own interests, curiosities and personal intelligence. The dead do not necessarily lay dormant just because they are ignored. This applies to dead information as well. Whether he likes it or not, or whether you or I like it or not, the Metamachine© is a vehicle of evolution. There are others who have worked on similar machines, too. One of them is the Navy, but that is another story. I do not think some of these other machines have anywhere near the capacity for the occult information that Joe has placed into his.

Although I have barely touched on the subject of the Metamachine©, it is not the subject of this book. It is mentioned a little bit, but many of Joe's fans had no real concept of what it was about. Sometimes those who knew about it became very possessive and tried to steal it or hack into Joe's regular computer in order to access information about it. This makes life uneasy, and while there are many tales that could be told, let us just say that this sort of behavior has induced Joe to retire to a place where he can hopefully enjoy the rest of his life. I have jokingly called him "Frodo Matheny" in reference to the Metamachine© being like the Ring of Power in *The Lord of the Rings*.

There has been considerable opposition to getting this book into your hands. If it has arrived, we have at least partly succeeded. More will be written on the development of the Metamachine© and how it came into being in a future book to be written by myself entitled *Synchronicity and the Seventh Seal: The Search for Ong's Hat*. This book will follow up on the threads presented in this narrative, but will also blow open my past research and experiences in synchronicity which accelerates the subject to a much higher level. Does it crack open the Seventh Seal of the Bible? You will have to wait and see, but I have used the analogy because it dispels the nonsense that has been salivated over in reference to that term. Opening the Seventh Seal is a personal process and will be experienced by different people in different ways and at different times. I certainly hope that our efforts here and in the future will expand your awareness. That is the promise. As it stands, the book is only partially written.

Another point that has been missed by many readers of *The Incunabula Papers* is the concept of the *Living Book*. What is the *Living Book*? It is a book which interfaces and interacts with the reader in much the same way that a virtual reality game would interface and interact with the player. It is a book which changes and evolves much the way that life adapts to the environment with evolution. It is a record of experiences, knowledge, and wisdom. That is the ultimate reference point of evolution and why Joe chose to build a Metamachine©. Life does not stop for one book. Life does not stop for Armageddon but swallows it, absorbs it and defines it according to its own image. Life moves on and on in the space of forever, in the realm of On, the creational vibration for which is known as Ong.

You have been searching for us without knowing it.

Peter Moon
Long Island, NY

Introduction

It is often said that life is stranger than fiction. Indeed, I can attest to that. However, how strange can life become when the lines between "truth" and "fiction" blur like a fractal basin boundary? Is reality elastic? Is the future co-creative? Can the endless possibility waves and bifurcation points along the seemingly linear flow of day-to-day life be codified and transmogrified? All good questions and my observations, experiments, and results over the last 10 years seem to point to the answer, *maybe*. Now, right now, you may be saying, all he concluded was *maybe*? To which I would have to answer, "I wasn't even sure of *that* when I began." Therefore the very possibility warrants further research in this area. That is not a failure, far from it.

What are the Incunabula/Ong's Hat documents and where did they come from? That's an interesting question and one I ask myself quite often. You see, even people who are neck deep into the Ong's Hat enigma can't quite answer that. So, where did this all come from? Well, there are 3 books (including this one) that will explain just that. That it will take 3 books to explain it all says something in and of its self. Here are the facts:

Where is Ong's Hat?

As Peter Moon said in a Spring 2001 ***Montauk Pulse*** article on the subject titled: *Ong's Hat and the Gateway to Parallel Worlds:*

> In the last issue of the *Pulse*, the story of Ong's Hat was introduced. Before we continue with that story, it will be interesting to backtrack and let everyone know what little historical facts have been gathered about this remote and enigmatic location in the Pine Barrens of southern New Jersey. Ong's Hat appears on some state maps but not on others. The designation appears just under thirty miles east of Philadelphia, just north of New Jersey State Highway 70. To arrive at the destination, you would take 70 to state highway 72 northwest and go up the road a couple of miles. There, you will find Ong's Hat Road and a bar in a little triangle. If you're lucky, some of the people in the bar might tell you some strange stories

about the area. The Pine Barrens themselves have always been a mysterious and enigmatic location. It was settled in the pre-revolutionary days and eventually included Hessians, the German soldiers paid by the British, who did not desire to return to their Germanic homeland. What little there is to learn of the history of Ong's Hat comes from Henry Beck who penned a book in 1936 entitled *Forgotten Towns of Southern New Jersey*. At that time, Ong's Hat had appeared on maps and been around for over a century, but no one had ever taken it too seriously. Mr. Beck took a photographer, a "State Editor" and traveled to the region and interviewed what remaining natives were left in the area that had been designated as Ong's Hat. According to them, the name originated from a young man whose last name was "Ong." Mr. Ong was quite a dancer who captivated the ladies with his smooth moves and fashionable and shiny high silk hat. At that particular time, the little village consisted only of small houses and a dance hall. There was also a clearing where semipro prizefights were held. It seemed that one Saturday night, Mr. Ong snubbed one of his female partners at which point she took the hat from his head and deliberately stamped upon it in the middle of the dance floor. Another account picks up the story at this point but offers a little more information. It was said that Mr. Ong, who was quite inebriated at the time, tossed his distinguished hat into a tree in the center of the village. There, it stood in the tree, unreachable and battered. It hung there amidst the rain and wind for many months. At some point, the little town acquired the name of Ong's Hat.

The Ong's Hat Ashram story, as told in the following chapters, seems to trace its roots back to the beginning of the Second World War. During the early post Pearl Harbor days of World War II, America suddenly found itself in the position of having its eastern seaboard invaded by German U-Boats and it's western seaboard invaded by Japanese submarines. Feeling behind in the race, so to speak, the military industrial complex was born and given carte blanche to proceed with any means necessary to get ahead in the war. From this initiative came many "secret projects" including the Ong's Hat project, the Montauk project, and more. The military got its brain power for a lot of these programs from Princeton University which is located very near Ong's Hat. See the current bestselling book and Hollywood movie, "*A Beautiful Mind*" for a mainstream look into that group of unique minds. Also, see the opening chapters to Neal Stephenson's *"Crytponomicon"*.

John Tukey was one of the many Renaissance minds that wandered in and out of the many official and unofficial groups that formed and reformed with the regularity and fluidity of a *Temporary Autonomous Zone*, as described by Hakim Bey. John Tukey attracted international attention for his studies in mathematical and theoretical statistics and their applications to a wide variety of scientific and engineering disciplines. He led the way in the now-burgeoning fields of Exploratory Data Analysis and Robust Estimation, and his contributions to the *Spectrum Analysis of Time Series* and other aspects of Digital Signal Processing have been widely used in engineering and science. He has been credited with coining the word "bit", a contraction of "binary digit", which refers to a unit of information, often as processed by a computer.

In addition to strong continuing interests in a wide variety of areas of statistical philosophy, techniques and application, Tukey was active in improving the access of the scientist to scientific literature, particularly through the development of citation and permutation indices to the literature of statistics and probability. Looking at an 11 April 1984 interview with John Tukey, we see this strange admission:

> **Tucker:** Wallman ended up as a professor of electric techniques at the Chalmers Institute in Gothenburg, Sweden, where he is now retired. He wrote a book with Witold Hurewicz on dimension theory.

> **Tukey:** It was intellectually about as strong a group as you are likely to find.

> **Tucker:** Wasn't Stone in this group?

> **Tukey:** Arthur, yes. When did Arthur come? He must have been here by '39. Arthur, Dick Feynman, Bryant Tuckerman—who went to IBM—and I were the people who invented hexaflexagons. This came about because Arthur had

an English-size notebook. Woolworth sold only American-size paper. He had to cut strips off the edges. He had to do something with the strips, so he started folding polygons. When he folded the hexagon he had the first hexaflexagon. Later came the Feynman diagram, the Tuckerman traverse, and so on.

Tucker: Was it that group that used the pseudonym "Pondiczery"?

Tukey: Yes, but with a somewhat broader reference.

Aspray: For what purpose?

Tukey: Well, the hope was that at some point Ersatz Stanislaus Pondiczery at the Royal Institute of Poldavia was going to be able to sign something ESP RIP. Then there's the wedding invitation done by the Bourbakis. It was for the marriage of Betty Bourbaki and Pondiczery. It was a formal wedding invitation with a long Latin sentence, most of which was mathematical jokes, three quarters of which you could probably decipher. Pondiczery even wrote a paper under a pseudonym, namely *"The Mathematical Theory of Big Game Hunting"* by H. Petard which appeared in the *Monthly*. There were also a few other papers by Pondiczery.

Tucker: Moulton, the editor of the *Monthly* at that time, wrote to me saying that he had this paper and the envelope was postmarked Princeton and he assumed that it was done by some people in math at Princeton. He said he would very much like to publish the paper, but there was a firm policy against publishing anything anonymous. He asked if I, or somebody else that he knew and could depend on, would tell him that the authorship would be revealed if for any reason it became legally necessary. I did not know precisely who they were, but I knew that John [Tukey] was one of them. He seemed to be in the thick of such things. John agreed that I could accept Moulton's terms. I sent a letter with this assurance to Moulton and he went ahead and published it. Which I thought was very flexible on ...

Tukey: Somebody with a high principle. Pondiczery's official residence was in *Ong's Hat, New Jersey* which is a wide place in the road going southeast from Pemberton, but it does appear on some road maps. There is a gas station that has a sign out about Ong's Hat.

Aspray: But no sign for Pondiczery?

Tukey: No sign for Pondiczery. Spelled c-z-e-r-y, by the way. Not like the area of India, Pondicherry, which is spelled c-h. Anyway, this was a good group, and I enjoyed its existence. I learned a lot from dinner table conversations. What was the name of our algebraist friend, a quiet soul who was around at that time?

To continue, further research into this area shows that the area of Ong's Hat was a popular weekend spot for the Princeton groups and has been used in a histiographic metafictional sense in this very context by Neal Stephenson, in his seminal work, *Cryptonomicon*. Keep the concept of the Ong's Hat Rod and Gun Club in your mind as you read this material (cited in the following chapters) and then think back to this sequence of clues when you encounter it. I think you will be able to put together the connection between a "Rod and Gun" club in Ong's Hat with the Princeton "weekender" phenomena and Tukey's "dinner club" reference above for yourself. To answer another question I'm sure you've just asked yourself, this was indeed the place and some of the people that became the group known as MJ-12.

So what does this mean? Well, it would seem to indicate that a group of scientists that were working on many secret projects wrote papers under pseudonyms and used the now deserted New Jersey Pine Barren Town of Ong's Hat as a "residence" address for this endeavor. Why would they do such a thing? In an interview I did with a man who claimed to have been a young technical writer for one of these teams (name withheld by request), some of the projects that the budding U.S. Military Industrial Complex were sponsoring may have, in the mind of the scientists, gotten into ethical "gray areas". Torn between duty to country and responsibility to the future of humankind, they "leaked" certain information to the general populace using the "fictional" character method. That they chose Ong's Hat for the residence of their fictional characters will become more suspicious as we progress. Also, the fact is that a big part of this team's focus was on cryptography and the cracking of the the Enigma codes. During World War II, one of these people, Alan Turing, served with the British "Government Communication Headquarters" (GCHQ) at Bletchley Park where he played a significant role in breaking the German "Enigma" codes. There, he used a machine called Collossus to decipher the Enigma codes. These machines were the predecessors to the first digital computers.

The scholastic sources that this amorphous and shadowy group drew upon, and the method of sending messages into the noosphere (as well as into the logos), within a coded document, will become even clearer later in this chapter. This method employs the technology known as memes as its primary force. Memes are patterns of information that behave like viruses. The science of memetics studies the replication, mutation, and carriers of memes. Many scientists consider memes to be actual living things that "ride" in the nervous systems of human beings, and hibernate in books, computer disks, etc. Examples of memes include catchy commercial jingles, the concept of money, political beliefs, and art styles. Certain memes, such as teenage cultural fads, are very susceptible to mutation, while others, such as the major religions, have hit evolutionary dead-ends and hardly change from decade to decade. Some memes, like fire building techniques, are beneficial to their host, while others are toxic to their host, such as the kamikaze and Jim Jones memes. Oxford zoologist Richard Dawkins coined the term meme in his 1976 book, *The Selfish Gene*. For now, hold those concepts as floating-point integers in your mind. The Princeton connection alone is interesting, but I site this comment as well, from Preston Nichols, famous as the person who broke the silence and secrecy on the Montauk Project:

In the **Spring 2001** edition of *The Montauk Pulse* Peter Moon wrote:

> In January of 1994, I was driving with Preston Nichols through the state of New Jersey. I hadn't gotten around to copying the data on Ong's Hat but told him a much-abbreviated version of the story you have just read. He looked at me and said that he had worked there for a short period. Apparently, he had been sent to do something there from his employer on Long Island. The secret government was involved in some capacity. He also said that Duncan Cameron had worked there extensively in an activity known as Project Dreamsleep. This has now been popularized in a movie called *Dreamscape*. Much of what Duncan did had to do with targeting then President Jimmy Carter (who was considered an enemy by at least one faction of the CIA — he wanted to cut its budget, reduce its staff, and make it more honest). I was all the more surprised when I sent the entire article to Madame X (mentioned in *Montauk Revisited*) and she said she used to get phone calls from these same people. There was no "normal" reason for them to call her at all. She said that she simply hears from people when she is supposed to. They were not good friends from the past or anything like that. When the nuclear accident occurred, she became very concerned as she never heard from them after that.

So, how does this all tie into the book catalog and the brochure? My first encounter with *Incunabula: A Catalog of Rare Books, Manuscripts & Curiosa* came about through serendipity. I was living in Santa Cruz, California at the time, having just moved from my childhood hometown of Chicago, Illinois, and had moved into a wonderful and affordable apartment building on a hill overlooking the beach. When I moved in, I discovered that former Millbrook, Esalen, UCSC, and ISC alumni were the primary inhabitants of the complex. Among these were Nina Graboi, former assistant to Timothy Leary at the Millbrook Institute in Duchess County New York, and assistant to UCSC

Chaos Mathematician Ralph Abraham; Bob Forte, friend and associate of Albert Hoffman, the inventor of LSD 25; and a plethora of similar "counter-culture" figures.

Becoming a resident of 321 Second Street acted as a nexus point for me. Nina was fond of entertaining various counter-culture figures as they came through central California in her "parlor". Eventually, a semi-organized group formed out of these salon sessions and took a name: the F.O.G., Formless Ocean Group. By way of association with Nina, Bob, and the F.O.G., I was brought into contact with many of the psychedelic figure heads of the time, like Terrence and Dennis McKenna, Peter Stafford, John Lilly, Dave Jay Brown, Elizabeth Gips, Paddy Long, Robert Anton Wilson, Timothy Leary, Nick Herbert, and Hakim Bey (aka, Peter Lamborn Wilson) to name a few.

One of the people I admired the most from The F.O.G. scene was Nick Herbert. Nick was a brilliant physicist who possessed a twisted sense of humor that I personally found palatable. Nick intrigued me for several reasons: he's funny and intelligent as hell, he had incredible stories about being convinced to walk out on the Livermore life by a "dimensional" being that he encountered, and his invention of the Metaphase Typewriter. The Metaphase Typewriter is a Quantum-uncertain text generator open for mediumistic possession by discarnate spirits.

WIRN OF ACERIONINE SE IND BE B WHAD ATHE OROVESSOUNDRO MAT PIND ASPAS HESUN UR D T CORE G LVIDESPANOUMO BIMARNAGLES HSTEAF NNAN A AITHIDIF PUTAMSUBENES T QUALOA ASELOTNULARE INE T THAPE ALLIGACAZOF WANE HT F A T G R ATHE FOVA WHISERDEM INOT ACRYRYIVESSTHENEMBOFO OR W WO WOMAD FORDISP AS HE WHA CO T T PLE F T OWRUS INIAIDITHE COR NITAL PIS D BEANSTOARERS THESITIVENOVERLASESTEWONM IST MIGHIPOF A DUNKISHENT ISEAD RIENDUBE THERROIN

The text above was created on a quantum-random typewriter overlain with second-order English language statistics. The "metaphase typewriter" was part of a project carried out by members of the Consciousness Theory Group to build machines to communicate with disembodied spirits, including spirits of the dead, and beings from other dimensions or dissociated fragments of living personalities.

Ordinary awareness is one of the biggest mysteries of our age: scientists are totally baffled by the fact that humans enjoy "inner experience" along with their behavior and are at a loss to explain the origin of this experience although much progress has been made in explaining the behavior. One small group of mind scientists believes that mind is a quantum effect and that disembodied entities (which might be called "souls") manipulate the body by willfully causing quantum possibilities to become actual. In this view mind enters the body from outside (a philosophical position known as "dualism") by operating on certain quantum-uncertain parts of the nervous system.

For centuries, special people have claimed to be possessed by discarnate beings, spirits of the dead, beings from other planets or higher dimensions. Members of the Consciousness Theory Group felt that there was something vaguely unethical about possessing an already occupied body and wondered if we could create an empty "consciousness-friendly" vessel and invite wandering souls to occupy it.

In the early 1970's Nick Herbert (SCM Corp) and Dick Shoup (Xerox PARC) designed and built the first "metaphase" devices— quantum operated machines that produced text (metaphase typewriter) and speech (quantum metaphone). We used for our quantum-uncertain source a quantity of radioactive Thallium monitored by a Geiger counter. We looked at the INTERVALS between Geiger counter clicks and printed a probable letter if that interval was very probable, printed an improbable letter if that interval was improbable (much longer than average, for instance). We obtained the second-order English language statistics from an unclassified NSA document available to the public.

The metaphase typewriter was operated under several curious conditions without much success. We invited several famous and not-so-famous psychics to try to influence the endless stream of random anagrams flowing from the typewriter or to cause the ghostly voice from the quantum metaphone to make sense in some known language. We held séances to evoke the spirits of colleagues who had recently died and who knew about the typewriter, and we held an all-day séance on the 100th anniversary of Harry Houdini's birth to try to contact the spirit of this great magician.

For the next step in metaphase research, I have proposed building quantum-driven communicators that are more consciousness-friendly than radioactive sources, devices that are more similar in size, operation and energy to the (purportedly) quantum synapses in human nervous systems. These devices, called "Eccles Gates" after Nobel laureate Sir John Eccles, one of the chief champions of quantum consciousness, would be composed of an array of quantum-uncertain silicon switches as much like the meat-based synaptic switches in our brains.

In the MPT experiments, I saw a mechanically scientific application of my theories on the construction of a "living book", and in my living book theories, which I will expound upon these in my next book, *Game Over?*, and in Peter Moon's next book, *Synchronicity and the Seventh Seal:The Search for Ong's Hat.* Nick saw an element that the MPT had been missing: namely, the human interface and magickal connection that seems to make this kind of stuff work. Also, with the results of the MPT experiment, I had methods, proofs, and failures to base my mathematical models that I was using as the framework for my Living Book.

During a session in my apartment, where we were smoking hash and deliberating the connections between the Quantum models for consciousness and a similar metaphor I had discovered while reading particular passage in James Joyce's *Ulysses*, Nick stopped me and pulled out a sheaf of Xeroxed papers from his bag.

"Ever see these?" he asked.

I picked up the papers and looked them over. "No," I replied. "Where did you get them?"

"Someone sent them to Felicia, anonymously," he replied.

I looked them over. Upon first glance it appeared to be a fringe science catalog, selling books. I pointed to my bookshelves.

"I have tons of this kind of stuff. I've been collecting fringe science pamphlets and booklets for years."

I then went to my bookshelf and pulled out a newly acquired copy of *High Weirdness by Mail.* I threw it down on the table.

"Look, someone even did a compendium of all the weird shit you can send away for," I said. "It's a fairly popular wacko pastime."

He snickered in the strange way that he had when he was being cryptically funny. "So, the fact that you have the compendium and a vast collection on your bookshelf of this stuff makes you one of the Alpha wackos, Joe?"

I laughed. "Yeah, I guess so!"

He pointed back to the catalog on the table. "I'm implicated in this. It says I wrote some book that was suppressed. Honestly, I didn't remember writing it until I read about it in here, but now I'm beginning to question if I did...."

We both stood comfortably silent as only the stoned can and stared at the catalog for a while.

A few days later, I was at a party at the Soundmotion Garden studios and I cornered Felicia, partly because I was genuinely interested in the origin of the catalog and partly because I thought Felicia was a total "hotty" (Californian for very attractive).

"Hey, did you get a weird Xerox catalog of science books and give it to Nick?" I asked.

"Oh, yeah, that. Yeah," she said.

"Where did it come from?" I asked.

"No idea, it came without a return address. How did you get it?" she replied.

"Nick..." I answered.

"Oh, yeah. Funny how all the books in that catalog are on your shelf, huh? I thought it might be from you..." she said smiling.

"Nope," I said. "I see how you could think that, but no."

I went inside from the deck. Nick was sitting in an overstuffed chair, holding wacko court as usual, with several Mondoids (followers of the radical publication Mondo 2000). I pulled him aside. "Still have that catalog you showed me the other day?" I asked.

"Yeah," he said as he reached into his bag and handed it to me. "Here. You can have it. I figure it's right up your alley."

I rolled it up and put it into my back pocket. I looked out the window and saw several German college tourist girls who had showed up at the party disrobing to enter the hot tub. I went back out to the deck and forgot about the catalog in my pocket for several days.

Days later, I pulled the catalog from my pocket as I prepared my pile of dirty clothes for the laundry. I read it as I waited for my laundry to finish in the apartment buildings community washing machine. I was stunned. This was so clever! Someone had actually disguised a brilliant short story as a crackpot book catalog! As a fan of Xerox crackpot lit, I could fully appreciate the methodology involved. I ran off several copies on a Xerox machine and gave them to several people. Eventually, utilizing a friend who owned one of the best-known mail order conspiracy book companies of the time, I set up a Xerox for cost edition. Individuals or other catalog companies would order sets and we would Xerox to order. I estimate that we distributed thousands like this. Later, when I began to look into the background and origins of the material, I discovered that this was no "joke" and, in fact, may represent a signal that is being transmitted in many different forms, all over time, whose full purpose I am yet to fully decipher although I have some very definite answers.

As you read the documents that follow, bear in mind that the catalog is not really a catalog, the brochure is not really a brochure. They are clever "enigma" codes that carry powerful symbolism, and a powerful message, disguised as a catalog and brochure.

Look no further than today's popular media to see the signal as it is picked up. At the time of the publication of this book, Fox network is running a wildly successful Saturday morning children's show called *Galidor*. The central theme of this show revolves around a transdimensional transport device called *The Egg*. There's even a plan to release a children's toy version of the Egg complete with an interdimensional traveling action figure appropriately named Nick.

A frequency, a signal, a message in a bottle?

Joseph Matheny

The following articles are extracteed from *The Montauk Pulse* by Peter Moon

WINTER PULSE 2000

There are many remarkable synchronicities I have encountered since putting *The Montauk Project: Experiments in Time* together with Preston Nichols. In the past, I have always thought they would fit into various books that I would write; however, there is no imminent opportunity to put any of these into book form at the current time. In the interest of posterity, and to stave off the possibility of losing the information thus researched, I am as of now going to commit as many of them as possible to *The Pulse*.

The following series of synchronicities I have to share concerns an enigmatic location in the Pine Barrens of New Jersey which is known as Ong's Hat. Although it appears on some maps, it has no designation on others. There is a rather elaborate website if you care to look it up on the internet at *www.incunabula.org*. It concerns time travel and other dimensional travel. My encounter with Ong's Hat occurred many years ago and long before the internet was available to me.

It was late in 1992 when I received a phone call from a man who claimed to represent an independent physics research group that had been studying Quantum Mechanics for some time. This man said that his group had John von Neumann's equations and were quite puzzled when they read *The Montauk Project*. They were not puzzled because they didn't understand it (they found it to be quite plausible except for maybe a few minor points) but because they couldn't believe why we omitted the information about von Neumann's equations. The answer was simple. Preston neither had them nor knew about them. This man eventually called Preston on the phone and questioned him for an hour. Finally, he convinced himself that Preston actually DID know what he was talking about.

Perhaps nothing more would have been made of all this except for a chance meeting I had in July of 1993 while staying at the Miller House inn located at the extreme western end of New York state in the little town of Sherman. A man checked into the inn under the name of Marshall Barnes. He woke up the next morning to find a copy of *The Montauk Project* sitting on a table in the inn. He asked the proprietor what he was doing with that particular book and was very surprised to find out I was staying at the same inn. To my surprise, Marshall introduced himself as being part of the physics group that had contacted us previously. We had a nice conversation and he spoke of a video project he was working on but he couldn't say too much about it. It had to do with interdimensional factors and he intimated that he had to lay low on the subject for a while. When I returned home, I received a phone call from Marshall informing me that I would soon be getting a package. It never came and I didn't hear from him for a long time. Why the package did not arrive had to do with some very mysterious circumstances. I will give you some background before I launch into what the package did contain.

In November of 1993, I was continuing my research into the Wilson/Cameron clan (as discussed in *Montauk Revisited*). At that time, I was very sensitive to any mention of a Cameron or Wilson when I noted that a lecture was being held in New York City by Peter Lamborn Wilson on the subject of Magick in Colonial North America. Attending Mr. Wilson's lecture on November 13th, I heard a rather scholarly account of how the settlers had suppressed native cultures and that history was written from the perspective of the winners. As a result, the heritage and wisdom of the "losing peoples" is lost. This was particularly true in the case of the Native American tribes of which the Montauk Indians are a prime example.

During a break, I introduced myself to Mr. Wilson and asked if he had heard of *The Montauk Project*. He said he had heard of the book but had not read it and needed to be reminded of what it was about. I then told him I was a "Wilson hunter" and why the name was important to me. He laughed as if he knew what I was talking about. I asked him if he had experienced any synchronicities or otherwise unusual circumstances that had to do with the names "Wilson" or "Cameron." Surprisingly, he had one. He said that one of the most fascinating characters he had ever come across was a Wilson who was run out of Scotland for being one of the most radical revolutionaries that country had ever known. He said the man ended up in America where he calmed down and became an ornithologist (one who studies birds). Mr. Wilson was very intrigued by the fact that one could be so involved in revolution and end up studying birds. It appeared so irregular. When I asked Mr. Wilson what this particular Wilson's first name was, he told me that it was "Alexander." This just happens to be the legal first name of Duncan Cameron, the time traveler from *The Montauk Project* who remembers being Marcus Wilson in an earlier life. Although this was too much of a coincidence to be taken lightly, I could not really take it any further.

The very next day, a little more information would trickle. I received a phone call from a man who said he was part of the Aviary Group. This is a code name for a front group for the CIA that studies, collects, and releases information concerning UFOs. It is not highly credible but the synchronicity with "birds" was interesting. The man who phoned me said he had grown up in Massachusetts next door to Marcia Moore (mentioned in *Montauk Revisited*) on one side and next door to a Wilson family on the other side. This coincidence was what he said prompted his call to me.

A few days later, I met with my psychic friend, Joy. She has experienced all sorts of synchronicities with the names "Cameron" and "Wilson" as stated in *Montauk Revisited*. To my surprise, she knew exactly why I was being pointed in the direction of birds. In fact, she said birds were highly intelligent and were her favorite animals. They are connected to the energy grids of the Earth. Homing pigeons and migrating birds tap this grid in order to know where they are going. It is a telepathic connection. The word "bird brain" is a misnomer. What they lack in size, they compensate for with telepathic ability. Scientific studies reported on in the *New York Times* reveal that parrots and other talking birds know what they are saying; however, most birds resent captivity and are either smart alecs or nonresponsive.

The meaning behind the bird connection would come full

circle when someone pointed out to me that the greatest bird in history was the Egyptian Phoenix who would renew itself in a funeral pyre every five hundred years. The name "Phoenix" is interesting because the Montauk Project itself was known as part of the "Phoenix Project." More importantly, I discovered that it was also the code name Aleister Crowley used as the head of the Ordo Templi Orientis. So, my search for Wilsons led me back to Crowley again. It reaffirmed his connection and allegorically implied that he was in a position over all the "birds" or "aviary group."

The above is background information and is terribly relevant to my own state of consciousness when I finally received the package that Marshall Barnes had promised me months earlier. Soon after the lecture by Peter Wilson, and right after my visit with Joy, I received the long awaited package. Inside were some very mysterious documents. First was a paper entitled "Ong's Hat" from a certain "P. Wilson." The first name, but not the first initial, was blackened out. I would later find out that the "P." was for Peter Lamborn Wilson.

The term "Ong's Hat" comes from a 19th century legend about a man named Ong who threw his hat up in the air and it never came down. Whether it landed in a tree or went into another world is the essence of the legend. Ong's Hat refers to the obscure location in the New Jersey Pine Barrens where some very secretive experiments took place that opened up a gateway to other worlds. All of this information appeared in a full color advertising brochure for the Institute of Chaos Studies and the Moorish Science Ashram in Ong's Hat, New Jersey.

The information in this brochure centered around startling new developments in Chaos Theory that occurred during the 1970's and 1980's that placed it on a level of importance with the subjects of Relativity and Quantum Mechanics. This new Chaos Theory was born out of mixing various different sciences including weather prediction, Catastrophe Theory, fractal geometry, developing computer graphics, hydraulics and fluid turbulence, evolutionary biology, mind/brain studies and psychopharmacology.

All of the above concerned progress in a field previously not contemplated by researchers in general. By the late 1980's, the Chaos Movement split into two hostile factions. One school placed emphasis on chaos itself, the other on order. The order people were known as Determinists and viewed chaos as an enemy. They interpreted the new theories as a vindication of Classical Newtonian physics. The opposing faction experienced chaos as something benevolent. It was viewed as the necessary matrix out of which creation arises spontaneously. This is the principle of the wild which these scientists viewed as vindication of Quantum indeterminacy and the promise of an open-ended universe. Chaos was viewed as healthy.

Predictably, the Determinists won the funding and support of the world governments and intelligence agencies. By the end of the 1980's, what was left of the Quantum/Chaos movement was forced underground after being virtually censored from prestigious scientific journals and large funding sources. Being on the edge, these dissidents found themselves part of the underground cultural chaos which included magicians, extremists and other anti-authority "mutants."

When leading theoreticians on Quantum/Chaos began to be fired from their university and corporate positions, they continued to pursue their goals and interest. A nebulous weave of pen-pals and computer networking arose. When the economic crash of 1987 happened, a vast but hard to view crack was opened in the social and economic control structures of America. Gradually these marginal characters began to fill up those fissures with a larger web of networking. Bit by bit, a genuine black economy arose along with a shifting and insubstantial but very influential "autonomous zone" which was impossible to map but real enough in its various manifestations. At this point, something began to crystallize. The influence of a New Aeon or magick in general could not be discounted. In order to get additional insight into these matters, we will next consider one particular case.

In 1913, a black circus magician named Noble Drew Ali founded an Islamic heretical sect and called it the Moorish Science Temple. In the 1950's, various jazz musicians and poets who belonged to this sect founded the Moorish Orthodox Church, tracing their spiritual ancestry to various "Wandering Bishops" loosely affiliated with the Old Catholic Church and schisms of Syrian Orthodoxy. In the 1960's, the Moorish Orthodox Church maintained a presence at Millbrook, New York at Timothy Leary's commune. Several members discovered Sufism and undertook journeys to the East. One such American, Wali Fard, travelled throughout Asia and collected exotic initiations in all sorts of different schools including the tantric arts and different forms of shamanism. At the same time he engaged in his spiritual journey, he traded in carpets and other well-known Afghan exports. The Soviet invasion induced him to return to America in 1978 whereupon he laundered his savings by buying about 200 acres in the New Jersey Pine Barrens. Around 1980, he moved into an old rod and gun club on the property along with several runaway boys from Paramus, New Jersey. An anarchist lesbian couple from Brooklyn joined them and together they founded the Moorish Science Ashram.

Through the early to mid-1980's, the communes fortunes fluctuated. Much experimentation ensued. After the Crash of '87, Moors and sympathizers sought refuge at the Ashram. Among the most notable were Frank and Althea Dobbs, twin brother and sister and also chaos scientists who had been fired from Princeton University (the home of the Philadelphia Experiment). The Dobbs twins grew up on a UFO-cult commune in Texas that was founded by their father, a retired insurance salesman who was murdered by "rogue disciples." As undergraduates at the University of Texas, the twins had produced a series of equations which they felt contained the seeds of a new science they termed "cognitive chaos." Their dismissal from Princeton was a result of their submitting these theorems, along with a theoretical/philosophical system built upon them, as a joint Ph.D. thesis.

Their theory was that brain activity could be modelled as a "fractal universe" of random and determined forces interfacing. Based upon this assumption, the twins showed that consciousness itself could be presented as a set of "strange attractors" (could also be called "patterns of chaos" or "coherent units of attractions") around which specific neuronal activity would organize itself. Keeping in mind that these attractors were not necessarily relegated to this dimension only, they sought patterns or "mind maps" through the actual geometry of the attractors themselves. By grasping these shapes both intuitively and non-intuitively, one could learn to "ride with chaos" much like a lucid dreamer learns to direct the process of REM sleep. Their aborted thesis suggested a mind boggling array of benefits such as links between cybernetic processes and awareness itself, including exploration of the brains unused capacities, awareness of the morphogenetic field and thus conscious control of autonomic functions such as repair of tissue and aging. Their thesis advisor told them that even the most modest of their proposals would suffice for expungement from the Graduate Faculty. If the whole concept was not such obvious lunacy, he would have reported them to the FBI as well.

Two more scientists already resided at Ong's Hat, and by sheer synchronicity, provided the perfect counterparts to the Dobbs twins' research. One was an expert in computers from Britain and the other was a Pine Barrens native who was an electronics buff who had set up a machine shop. The synergy at the Institute for Chaos Studies or ICS exceeded all expectations. Contacts with other underground experts were maintained by "black modem" as well as personal visits. The environment was both scientific and natural and included a hodgepodge of Tantra, Sufism, Ismaili esotericism, alchemy, psychopharmacology, biofeedback and brain machine meditation techniques. All of this harmonized beautifully with the "pure science" of the ICS. Under these conditions, progress proved amazingly swift, stunning everyone. Within a year, major advances had been made in all the fields predicted by the equations. After more than three years, the major breakthrough had occurred which would reorient the entire project in a new direction: THE GATE.

The development of The Gate began with the communities concern for consciousness and the enlargement of mental, emotional and psychic activities. This began with the meditation techniques W. Fard had learned in Central Asia and the first generation psychotronic devices developed during the 1980's. Exotic pharmacology was also involved. After the first successes of the Dobbs' research, the spiritual knowledge of the Ashram was reorganized into a preparatory course in "Cognitive Chaos." All workers were trained in this and the consciousness of the community became a practical extension of the theories and community that had evolved up to that point. Thus, the theorems were abstracted into literal contemplation of the community. They were one in the mind of the group and the individuals. This was all part of the process of "refining attention." At the same time, a "psychic anchor" was constructed by means of a firm grounding in celebratory body awareness. This is through the means of the tantric arts which refers to the erotic or sensual faculties being aimed at a higher plateau. These states of ecstasy are the ground on which the sacred dance of life is performed.

There was a second course administered to the workers which involved practical instruction in the hard sciences from genetics to brain physiology, Quantum Mechanics and computers. These subjects were tailored for the relevance at hand.

After this indoctrination, a fellow of the ICS was ready for a device called the "egg." This consisted of a modified sensory deprivation chamber in which attention could be focused on a computer terminal and screen. Electrodes were taped to various body parts to provide physiological data which was fed into the computer.

The explorer would then don a highly sophisticated helmet which was a fourth generation version of the early brain machines. This could sonically stimulate brain cells either locally or globally and in various combinations, thus directing not only brain waves but also highly specific mental/physical functions. The helmet was also plugged into the computer and provided feedback in various programmed ways. The explorer would then undertake a series of exercises in which the theorems were used to generate graphic animations of the "strange attractors" which map the various states of consciousness. From this setup, feedback loops were established between this "iconography" and the actual states themselves which were in turn generated through the helmet simultaneously with a representation being viewable on the computer screen. Certain exercises involved the "alchemical" use of mind active drugs (vasopressin derivatives, beta-endorphins, and hallucinogens usually administered in threshold dosages).

At the outset of the entire project, and despite censure from the academic community, the ICS founders realized that the Dobbs twins' research predictions were probably cautious or conservative. Enhanced control of autonomous body functions were attained early on even down to the cellular level. Certain unexpected side effects occurred which would usually be classified as paranormal. It was no longer a question of hallucination. Measurable results were attained not only in terms of "yogic powers" (suspended animation, lucid dreaming and the like) but also in observable benefits to health like rapid healing and remission of chronic conditions.

At this point in the development of the egg (which was the third generation), the researchers attempted to "descend" to the Quantum level. They sought to reach the state of consciousness where a wave becomes a particle. If this occurred at the moment of observation, it implied that human consciousness is involved in the actual Q-structure of reality itself. They hoped to attain this by "riding the wave" in an attempt to experience (rather than observe) the wave collapse into a particle. After months of research, none of the "Quantum travellers" experienced such an occurrence. It was realized according to J. Wheeler (of the Everett-Wheeler Hypothesis fame), that the wave function need never collapse provided that every Q-event gives rise to an alternative world (this is known to Quantum scientists as an instance of Schrödinger's cat being both alive and dead). They decided to test this further.

This concludes part one of the Ong's Hat saga as told in my own words. The next part will finish this story and add more to the mix from new data I have encountered. The plan ultimately is to reveal how this project connects to the Montauk Project. Tune in for the Spring 2001 issue.

In the last issue of the *Pulse*, the story of Ong's Hat was introduced. Before we continue with that story, it will be interesting to backtrack and let everyone know what little historical facts have been gathered about this remote and enigmatic location in the Pine Barrens of southern New Jersey. Ong's Hat appears on some state maps but not on others. The designation appears just under thirty miles east of Philadelphia, just north of New Jersey State Highway 70. To arrive at the destination, you would take 70 to state highway 72 northwest and go up the road a couple of miles. There, you will find Ong's Hat Road and a bar in a little triangle. If you're lucky, some of the people in the bar might tell you some strange stories about the area.

The Pine Barrens themselves have always been a mysterious and enigmatic location. It was settled in the pre-revolutionary days and eventually included Hessians, the German soldiers paid by the British, who did not desire to return to their Germanic homeland. What little there is to learn of the history of Ong's Hat comes from Henry Beck who penned a book in 1936 entitled *Forgotten Towns of Southern New Jersey*. At that time, Ong's Hat had appeared on maps and been around for over a century, but no one had ever taken it too seriously. Mr. Beck took a photographer, a "State Editor" and travelled to the region and interviewed what remaining natives were left in the area that had been designated as Ong's Hat. According to them, the name originated from a young man whose last name was "Ong." Mr. Ong was quite a dancer who captivated the ladies with his smooth moves and fashionable and shiny high silk hat. At that particular time, the little village consisted only of small houses and a dance hall. There was also a clearing where semipro prize fights were held. It seemed that one Saturday night, Mr. Ong snubbed one of his female partners at which point she took the hat from his head and deliberately stamped upon it in the middle of the dance floor. Another account picks up the story at this point but offers a little more information. It was said that Mr. Ong, who was quite inebriated at the time, tossed his distinguished hat into a tree in the center of the village. There, it stood in the tree, unreachable and battered. It hung there amidst the rain and wind for many months. At some point, the little town acquired the name of Ong's Hat. This was the location allegedly chosen for space-time experiments, as discussed in the last *Pulse*, by the Institute for Chaos Studies and the Moorish Science Ashram. At Ong's Hat, these mysterious and enigmatic cohorts allegedly produced an "egg" or vessel which was equipped as a sort of sensory deprivation chamber in which attention could be focused on a computer terminal and screen. With electrodes placed on the body to provide physiological data fed into the computer, as well as a helmet which stimulated brain cells in various combinations, the explorer undertook a series of exercises which generated graphic animations of "strange attractors" which mapped various states of consciousness in the individual. When the fourth generation of the egg evolved, it was simultaneously tested at the same time that a burst of research was carried out in the abstruse areas of Hilbert space and the topology of n-dimensional geometry on the intuitive assumption that new "attractors" could thereby be generated and used to visualize or "grok" the transitions between alternate universes. In other words, the geometry of infinite dimensions was contemplated against a scientific background so as to give the explorer a concept of an attractor that would or might lead to a transition to another dimension. Success was attained but only after an unmatched moment of fear and panic. On the Spring Equinox, one of the original Paramus runaways named "Kit" did a run through. The entire egg vanished from the laboratory. Everyone freaked out, but after seven minutes, the egg reappeared with Kit beaming like the Cheshire Cat. He had succeeded in riding the wave to its "destination," an alternate universe. He had observed it and in his words "memorized its address." Instinctively, Kit felt that certain dimensional universes must act as "strange attractors" in their own right and are thus far easier to access (more "probable") than others. In other words, he had not been dissolved but had found the way to a universe next door. The Gateway had been opened. As could be expected with such a remarkable breakthrough, trouble soon began to surface. It just so happens that Ong's Hat is located just south of the South Jersey Nuclear Waste Dump near Fort Dix. A major nuclear accident made this obscure area even more empty and unpopular. An electrified fence now shuts off the nuclear forbidden zone which is less than a mile from the ICS area. Despite the accident, the ICS stuck it out and combatted radiation sickness with their own technology. They resolved to stay until the "authorities" proved too hot to endure. Once the Gate was discovered, an interdimensional doorway had been opened. A full scouting occurred in the next dimension. It was an area just like New Jersey except that the entire planet seemed never to have developed human life. Little by little, the entire research center of the ICS was moved to the next dimension with trips back to our world. There was much dependence on the creature comforts of our world and on technology like computers. Does all of this mean that this new world must be colonized by the ICS? If so, how? Unfortunately, we are left with this question as this is where the story ends. The original publication was presented like a New Age vacation brochure embedded with enough clues for its intended readers (who are already halfway to Ong's Hat in any case) to pursue but not enough for those of little reality or perception to follow. Although this is where the brochure ended, it is not where my story ends.

In January of 1994, I was driving with Preston Nichols through the state of New Jersey. I hadn't gotten around to copying the data on Ong's Hat but told him a much abbreviated version of the story you have just read. He looked at me and said that he had worked there for a short period. Apparently, he had been sent to do something there from his employer on Long Island. The secret government was involved in some capacity. He also said that Duncan Cameron had worked there extensively in an activity known as Project Dreamsleep. This has now been popularized in a movie called *Dreamscape*. Much of what Duncan did had to do with targeting then President Jimmy Carter (who was considered an enemy by at least one faction of the CIA he wanted to cut its budget, reduce its staff, and make it more honest).

I was all the more surprised when I sent the entire article to

Madame X (mentioned in *Montauk Revisited*) and she said she used to get phone calls from these same people. There was no "normal" reason for them to call her at all. She said that she simply hears from people when she is supposed to. They were not good friends from the past or anything like that. When the nuclear accident occurred, she became very concerned as she never heard from them after that.

In April of 1994, I was attending an Anti-Gravity Conference in Philadelphia with Marshall Barnes, the man who had sent me the story of Ong's Hat. He was selling a series of notes. As I sat at a table, he demonstrated how refraction of light results in invisibility. Picking up his notes, I saw a copy of the same publication he had originally sent to me about Ong's Hat. As was said in the last issue of the *Pulse*, it was authored and/or presented by a "P. Wilson" with the first name, except for the "P" being blacked out. In this publication, however, the name was no longer blacked out. It read, "Peter Lamborn Wilson," the very same man I had met the previous November. When I called him on it, Marshall was apologetic and said he was sorry that he could not tell me everything. He further explained that he wanted to contact Peter Lamborn Wilson but did not want me or anyone else to spoil it.

According to Marshall, he had investigated the entire matter of Ong's Hat as thoroughly as he could. The entire story had been attributed to Peter Lamborn Wilson who had claimed it was all a hoax. Marshall said that the entire story is too logically put together and that there is too much corroborating evidence to dismiss it as a hoax. He said the names were changed and that he also knew a lot more that he could not tell me at that point. The fact that I met Peter Lamborn Wilson and that he did not mention a word of any of this is highly ironic, especially when you consider the fact that I was telling him about a space-time project. It has also been pointed out that Mr. Wilson may not even be aware of his own serious involvement in such a project. When I told him that the name Wilson was synonymous with time phenomena, he at least did provide some interesting clues.

Although that is where my investigation stood in 1994, there have been considerable developments since that time which will eventually be included in a book which is in progress and tentatively entitled *The Search for Ong's Hat*. Since that time, I have seen Peter Lamborn Wilson lecture at least twice and have given him a copy of *The Montauk Project*. It was subsequently featured in New York City on a broadcast of the Moorish Orthodox Church. When I told him that I knew someone who had determined that the Ong's Hat travel brochure had too much relevant and accurate information in it to be a simple hoax, he smiled and said that he was very impressed; however, he issued an official "no comment" in front of the audience. At some point, I did a major double-take when I looked at his middle name and realized that it is "Lamborn," a very remarkable pun on the idea of Lam-born. Remember, Lam was the grey-headed creature contacted by Crowley in 1918 before he set out to Montauk Point. Lam said, "it is all in the egg," a sychronistic allusion to the egg device used at Ong's Hat. Asking Peter Wilson where his middle name came from, he told me that no one in his family was quite certain about the true history of the name except that it seemed to be derived from a town in England by the name of Lambourn.

Last year, I met an old associate of Peter Wilson's by the name of Joe Matheny, the man who is primarily responsible for circulating the legend of Ong's Hat via the internet and has recently produced a CD-ROM on the subject which is available from Sky Books. There are many synchronicities we have shared with each other which will intensify the one's you have already read about by at least a hundredfold and probably much more. I have a LOT more to tell and further investigation will prove very interesting.

Autumn Pulse 2001

World Trade Center and Ong's Hat
It has been said that years from now everyone will remember exactly what they were doing when they learned of the attack on the World Trade Center. Well, guess where I was? I had just set out for an investigation of Ong's Hat. This trip was to inaugurate my next work, tentatively entitled *The Search for Ong's Hat*.

Setting off after 9:00 o'clock, I made my way down the parkways and turned on the radio in order to hear a traffic report. As two of my friends were conversing, I heard the announcement that a plane had crashed through a tower. As we listened for more information and entered the Belt Parkway in Brooklyn, we could see the two towers ablaze with a cloud of smoke that went on for miles. As my friend studied the blaze with his binoculars, we passed around a ridge as the towers collapsed. Then, we could see only smoke. On the radio, we heard that planes had crashed at the Pentagon and at Camp David. I tried to get off Long Island and continue with our trip, but the Verrazano Bridge, which goes from Brooklyn to Staten Island, was closed. We had to return home, and I never made it to Ong's Hat.

I had to wonder about the synchronicity of the whole event as my last plans to visit Ong's Hat were in March and they were subverted by another occurrence. It is obvious that some synchronicity was making itself known, but it took a long time to sink in. I heard stories that a group called the "White Knights," a conglomeration of "good guys" in the Government and in other key sectors of society were meeting in the World Trade Center at the time of the attacks. An extension of this group was also in the Pentagon at the exact location where it was hit. These people were allegedly working at the highest level of government and were going to revamp the economic system and put it on something like a gold standard. It has also been pointed out by structural engineers that the World Trade Center collapsed exactly as if demolition charges had been placed within it. Structural engineers are not buying what the media has offered as an explanation for the collapse of the towers. It is also a fact that the head of security for the World Trade Center was murdered just ten days before this occurence. This was reportedly done during a street robbery, the suspect of which is in custody. None of these matters have been examined in detail or been debated in the media. We have been steered away from any conspiracy theories. The seed for the "White Knights" theory was planted before September 11th and you can look that up on the internet for further information. I do not know if it is all true and am not going to focus on it. Instead, I think there are more pertinent observations to be made with regards to the recent attacks and how they tie into Ong's Hat.

According to the original legend, the community at Ong's Hat was built upon the foundations of the Moorish Science Temple and the Moorish Orthodox Church, both of which are considered heretical Moslem sects. Whether it is true or not, one of the most incredible stories of Ong's Hat concerns Wali Fard, an African-American from Chicago who is a legend in his own right. After traveling throughout Asia and experiencing exotic initiations from different mystery schools, Fard amassed a fortune from trading in carpets and other well known Afghan exports (we can assume hashish and opium). The Soviet invasion of Afghanastan induced him to return to America in 1978. Fard laundered his earnings by buying about 200 acres in the New Jersey pine barrens and set up the foundation for that which became known as the Institute for Chaos Studies and the Ong's Hat legend.

Remember, it was Peter Lamborn Wilson who played an integral role in purveying this information through channels which came to me. Although many of you may not know it, Peter Wilson is a major figure in the counter- culture where he is better known by his pseudonym of Hakim Bey. He has produced some fascinating works on Islam, a summary of which is in his book entitled *Sacred Drift*. A man who once served as an interpreter for the Shah of Iran, Peter Wilson is also a member, and some say secret sponsor, of the Moorish Orthodox Church.

Next, I would like you to consider the terrorist attacks and how the term "Islamic fanatic" has become a totally accepted idiom and explanation by our culture. When it comes to assassinations, "Islamic fanatic" is much less suspicious than "the lone nut theory." As revolting as it was, the terrorist attack on America was one of the most excellently executed and well planned attacks in the history of modern warfare, especially when you consider the resources of the terrorists. They are clearly in the position of the underdog, but they are absolutely fearless in their resolve. The media, in their ignorance if not their deliberate will to disinform, has neglected to zero in on the heart of the matter. First, it takes a lot of mind control to induce one to give up one's life. Most mind control agents, such as Mark David Chapman and John Hinckley, either botch up the job or leave a messy trail behind them. This was not an ordinary "intel job," however, we can pause and think about what exactly is the common denominator between mind control and Arab terrorists. The answer is, of course, the Nazis. The Lords of the Black Stone were mentioned in *The Black Sun* as being one of the most powerful secret societies in the world. They revere the black stone in Mecca as their symbol, and one of their agents, Otto Skorzeny, brought Arab terrorism to the modern world by training terrorists in Egypt in the '50's.

President Bush has pandered to Islam by acknowledging it as a great religion. The media has piggybacked on this theme and has sought to educate ignorant Americans on the idea that there are "good Muslims" and "bad Muslims." This is something akin to taking away a Native American's way of life, putting him in a Sunday suit, giving him a Bible, and teaching him how to be a "good Indian." We are not dealing with good or bad Muslims. We are dealing with an ancient society known as the Ismailis.

A thousand years ago in Cairo, the Ismailis ran one of the most successful and abundant mystery schools in the modern era. They were renown for their teaching and educational accomplishments. Under the political intrigue of the day, they were deposed and a different faction of Islam ruled in Egypt. The Ismailis went underground after that and have retained a base in Cairo which still exists to this day. Although their roots remained as an underground movement, they received their most public notoriety in the 11th Century when a Persian by the name of Hasan Sabbah reinvigorated the movement and established a remote outpost at Mount Alamut in Iran. Although he is often referred to as the Grand Master of the Assassins or the Old Man of the Mountain, he was only known in his own time as "the Master." He is an actual historical character who Marco Polo commented upon during his travels. Popular legends have him drugging young men and transporting them to a "garden of delights" in order to convince them that they were in heaven. By such stimulus-response conditioning, advocates believed that they would reach paradise if they followed the will of the master. (Ironically, Peter Wilson has been known to frequent, some say sponsor, a coffee house in Brooklyn called "Garden of Delights".) Hasan Sabbah was one of the most influential and pervasive people of his time and used assassination as the most expedient political tool of the day. Despite great odds, he subordinated the entire area of the planet in which he lived. According to a legend with much historical merit, he convinced an approaching Christian army to leave him alone by merely giving a hand signal to one of his devotees who was perched over a high drop. Upon receiving the signal, the man willingly jumped to his death upon the craggy rocks below. Whatever the reason or the motivation, Hasan Sabbah had mastered men's minds through the principles of devotion and sudden death.

The popular press has characterized Osama bin Laden as the mastermind behind the terrorist attacks. In actuality, it is far more complicated. We are dealing with a secret society that goes back thousands of years and might take ten, twenty or even one hundred years to put an assassin in place to commit an execution. This modus operandi is the gravest danger for the United States of America at this particular time. The terrorists could not have hit a more significant symbol than the trade towers. The only way for them to hit a more dramatic target and to strike terror into the heart of America would be for a carefully placed assassin to strike at the heart of the President himself. This means a person who is very close to him. This would be the most demoralizing act we could suffer as a nation. Whether it plays out or not, and I certainly hope it does not, this is how this sect works. One of the top programmer/hackers in the world is an Arab with sympathies to the terrorists. He facilitated an intimidating message to the White House when the terrorists revealed to our government that they knew exactly where the President was at the time of the attacks because they had broken the security codes. They were sending a message to the President himself.

The overall picture is very complicated, and it is too easy to over simplify, especially when we consider the nature of Islam

57

versus the way it is portrayed by the popular press. Islam and its most holy relic, the Kaaba, have long been described by some as a repository for negative energy. In this sense, negative does not mean "bad." Negativity is part of the constructs of life and symbolizes the dual nature of the universe. In most dichotomies, the female energy has usually been positioned as "negative." In Islam, they use the crescent moon as their symbol and follow the lunar calendar. These are both feminine symbols. Their holy day is Friday, the day of Freya or Venus. The Kaaba, which means cave, is also feminine. Of course, women have long been abused in the Arab world. When we consider a female as negative polarity (as opposed to a male or positive polarity), extreme negativity (the negating of the negative) results in annihilating the female. This is exactly what the Montauk Project did. It is the most negative of the negative.

Gaia, or Mother Earth, has long been under assault by patriarchal institutions which pillage and exploit the Third World. The international community has for a long time thought of the U.S. as a regime which supports, through the CIA, puppet dictatorships which ignore and hurt the population of the Earth. Statistically, over half of the world is literally starving, a blatant abandonment of the Earth's children. One of the worst things you can do to a woman is to abuse her children. It will garner the most explosive of responses. This is what the huge protests over the World Trade Organization were about. The World Trade Center was thus a symbolic target for annihilation. This horrible tragedy almost pales in comparison to Mother Earth's billions who suffer without any succor.

Do not think for a minute that the Assassins do not know this. They know negativity better than we do as they live and breathe it. It is in their blood and they are willing to perform the supreme sacrifice. This does not mean that the Assassins are doing this for Mother Earth, but, in a way, they are doing her bidding. Food packages are being airlifted en masse over Afghanastan. The relationship between Mother Earth and the Assassins is far too complicated to examine here, but the Goddess, in such forms as Kali, will employ very dark forces in order to carry out her desires or intention.

We get more insight into the bizarre associations of the Assassins when we consider that virtually all serious studies of the Ismailis (their real name) mention that they imparted their wisdom (identified as Sophia — the female principle) to the Knights Templar and were actually the foundation of that highly secretive and successful organization. The grail romances of the day always included a Saracen (one of the Islamic faith) who carried the standard of wisdom and was the bearer of light amidst the darkness that had descended upon Europe during the Inquisition. The relationship between the Templars and Assassins is a fascinating one, but the latter never referred to themselves by that name. Assassins is an appendage originally used by the Crusaders. Etymologists have long said that the term Assassins derives from hashishins because it was believed that hashish was the key ingredient used in the programming of devotees. This etymology has now come into question by certain scholars. Regardless of its correctness, the last datum caused me to have a look of my own at the word *assassin*. I could not help but notice that the word *ass* appears twice. This is synchronistic but first I must tell a little story.

It is very well known that the Templars participated in bizarre rituals and worshipped a strange head. This is sometimes referred to as Baphomet but more commonly as the head of an ass and also a donkey's head. Whatever the description, it is usually quite abhorrent. This is also where the expression "kiss my ass" comes from as this is literally what certain Templars were expected to do, sometimes to a human ass. It was an act of conformity to the order.

Going back to the etymology of the word *ass*, the Webster's *New Universal Unabridged Dictionary* indicates that this word is probably a hypocoristic (meaning a pet name or term of endearment) for the Old Irish word *asan*. This word is simply a different spelling of Hasan, the first name of Hasan Sabbah, the leader of the Assassins. There are several implications here. Most obvious is that when the Templars worshipped or acknowledged the ass, they were paying homage to Hasan. It is also possible that Hasan was only the human embodiment of an even older entity known as "Hasan." When Jesus road a virgin ass into Jerusalem, it was a very important part of an ancient ritual. The ass or donkey is also a well known symbol for the beast or Antichrist. The ancient Jews worshipped a god named Iao which is a personal name for or derived from YWHW or Yahway (instead of Jehovah). In the Coptic language of Egypt, Io or Eio means "donkey." This ancient Jewish worship is thought to have derived from the ancient Egyptian worship of Set or Seth who was the god of foreigners. Of course, the Egyptians equated the Jews as foreigners so ascribed this attribute to them. Seth was a villain to the Egyptians and used what could be described as "donkey magic."

Looking up the word *donkey* was the most interesting of all. According to the above dictionary, this word is a variant of Dunkey, a pet variant of the name Duncan. *Webster's New World Dictionary* also has this word deriving from Duncan, but with a question mark. Of course, Duncan is the mysterious time traveler from *The Montauk Project*. More intrigue is added to the mix when we consider that the Scottish Freemasons, who received their wisdom from the Templars, use the "Duncan Rituals" as part of their tradition to this very day. I have also seen Duncan Cameron react quite viscerally when the subject of the Templars is brought up. All of this would indicate that we are dealing with a consciousness that seeks to regulate the continuum and one that resonates with the experience known as the Montauk Project.

This catalog is a reproduction. This is not a commercial advertisement. Consider this an unusually complete bibliography to the story that unravels in the companion documents. Read this like a short story and you will agree with us that it is in fact a coded message and not a book catalog at all. For the purpose of historical preservation we have left any typos and mispellings from the original intact.

INCUNABULA

A Catalogue of Rare Books, Manuscripts & Curiosa
Conspiracy Theory Frontier Science & Alternative Worlds
Emory Cranston, Prop.

Incunabulum/cocoon/swaddling clothes/cradle/ incunae,
in the cradle/koiman, put to sleep/winding-sheet/koimetarium
(cemetery)/printed books before 1501, hence by
extension any rare & hermetic book...

INTRODUCTION

No book for sale here was actually printed before 1501, but they all answer to the description "rare and hermetic" — even the mass market paperbacks, not to mention the Xeroxes of unpublished manuscripts, which cannot be obtained from any other source!

The symbol INCUNABULA was chosen for our company for it's *shape*-cocoon; egg-like, gourd-like — the shape of Chaos according to Chaung Tzu. Cradle: beginings. Sleep: dreams. Silken white sheets of birth and death; books, white pages, the cemetery of ideas.

This catalogue has been put together with a purpose: to alert YOU to a vast cover up, a conspiracy so deep that no other researcher has yet become aware of it (outside certain Intelligence circles, needless to say!) — and so dangerous that the "winding sheet" imagery in our title seems quite appropriate; we know of *at least* two murders so far in connection with this material.

Unlike other conspiracy theories, such as Hollow Earth, Men In Black, cattle mutilation, UFO, Reich & Tesla or what have you, the INCUNABULA Theory harmonizes with genuine frontier quantum mechanics and chaos mathematics, and does not depend on any quack nostrums, psuedoscience or ESP for proof. This will become clear to anyone who takes the trouble to read the background material we recommend and offer for sale.

Because of the unprecedented nature of the INCUNABULA File we have included short descriptions of some of the books, pamphlets, flyers, privately — circulated or unpublished manuscripts, ephemera & curiosa available through us. Some of this is highly inflammable and sexual in nature, so an age statement must be included with each order.

Cash (or stamps) only. No cheques or money orders will be accepted.

Thank You,
Emory Cranston, Prop.

1. Wolf, Fred Alan
Parallel Universes: The Search for Other Worlds
(New York, Simon & Schuster, 1988)

Written by a scientist for non-scientists, simplistic and jokey, makes you feel a bit talked-down-to. Nevertheless Wolf uses his imagination (or other scientist's imaginations) so well he seems to hit accidentally on certain truths - (unless he knows more than he reveals). For example: the parallel universes must have all come into being simultaneously "at the beginning" in order for quantum uncertainty to exist, because there was *no observer* present at the Big Bang, thus no way for the Wave Function to collapse and produce one universe out of all the bubbles of possibility (p. 174). If an electron can disappear in one universe and appear in another (as suggested by the Everett/Wheeler material), a process called "quantum tunneling", then perhaps *information* can undergo a similar tunneling effect. Wolf suggests (p.176) that this might account for certain "psychic phenomenon, altered states of awareness", even ghosts and spirits! Actual travel between worlds must of course involve tunneling by both electrons AND information — any scientist would have predicted as much — but the mention of "altered states" of consciousness is *extremely revealing*! Elsewhere (p.204), Wolf speculates that a future "highly developed...electronic form of biofeedback" will allow us to observe quantum effects in the electrons of our own bodies, making the enhanced consciousness and the body itself a "time machine" (which is what he calls a device for travel between universes). He comes so close to the truth then shies away! For instance (p.199) he points out that the Wave Function has a value BETWEEN zero and one until it collapses. If the wave function does not collapse, the "thing" it describes exists in two universes simultaneously. How strange of him not to mention that fractal geometry also deals with values between zero and one! As we know the secret of travel between worlds is rooted in the marriage of quantum and chaos, particularly in the elusive mathematics of *fractal tesseracts* (visualize a 4-dimension Mandelbrot Set — one of the simplest of the trans-dimensional "maps" or "catastrophic topologies"). Wolf appears so unaware of this, we must sadly conclude that he's not part of the conspiracy.

Particularly interesting — and not found in any other material — are Wolf's speculations about schizophrenia. Are schizophrenics receiving information from other worlds? Could a schizoid observer actually observe (in the famous double slit experiments) a wave becoming two particles and then one particle? Or could such an observation be made by an extremely blank and simple-minded watcher (a sort of Zen simpleton perhaps)? If so, the perfect subject for parallel-worlds experiments would be a paradoxically complex simpleton, a "magnetized schizophrenic" who would be aware of the split into two worlds which occurs when a quantum measurement is made. Oddly enough, such a mental state sounds very close to the "positive schizophrenia" of certain extreme psychedelic experiences as well as the meditation-visualization exercises of actual travelers between worlds.

Despite it's flaws, an essential work.

2. Herbert, Nick
Quantum Reality
(NAL,1986)

A masterful and lucid exposition of the different versions of reality logically describable from various interpretations of quantum mechanics. The Everett/Wheeler Theory is here given the clearest explanation possible in lay persons terms, given the authors awareness (at the time) of experimental verification.

3. ibid.
Faster Than Light: Superluminal Loopholes in Physics
(NAL,1988)

Some of the theorists who touch on the Many-Worlds "hypothesis" place too much emphasis on time distortions and the implication of "time travel". These of course seem present in the theorems, but in practice have turned out (so far) to be of little consequence. Chaos Theory places much more emphasis on the temporal directionality than most quantum theory (with such exceptions as R. Feyman and his "arrow of time"), and offers strong evidence for the past-present-future evolution that we actually experience. As K. Sohrawardi puts it, "the universe is in a state of Being, true, but that state is not static in the way suggested by the concept of 'reversibility' in Classical physics. The 'generosity' of Being, so to speak, is becoming, and the result is not reversibility but multiplicity, the immeasurable resonant chaos — like fecundity of creation." Nevertheless, Herbert's second book is a brilliant speculative work — and it led him directly to a certain circle of scientists and body of research concerned with dimensional travel, rather than "time travel", with the result that his third book (see next item) finally struck pay-dirt.

4. "Jabir ibn Hayaan" (Nick Herbert).
Alternate Dimensions
(publication suppressed by Harper & Row,1989)
bound   uncorrected galleys, 179pp.

While working on *Faster Than Light* Herbert came into contact with one of the "travel cults" operating somewhere in California, perhaps one with a sufiistic slant ("Jabir ibn Hayaan" was a famous 10th century sufi alchemist); according to the preface of *Alternate Dimensions*, which is irritatingly vague and suggestive, this group seems to have trained him and sent him on at least one trip to America2. Herbert suggests that he already had so much experience of altered states of consciousness and ability to visualize complex space/time geometries that only a minimum of "initiatic" training proved necessary.

In any case, despite it's vagueness and brevity, this book is the most accurate and thoroughly-informed work on travel between worlds in our entire collection. So far we have been unable to obtain any *deep* theoretical work, and only a few papers dealing with practical aspects — but Herbert provides a magnificent overview of the entire field. Written for the lay person, with his usual clear and succinct approach to theory, Herbert's is the first "popular" study to make all the basic links: the Everett/ Wheeler hypothesis, Bell's Theorem, the E/R Bridge, fractal geometry and chaos math, cybernetically-enhanced biofeedback, psychotropic and shamanic techniques, crystallography, morphogenetic field theory, catastrophe topology, etc.

Of course he's strongest in discussing the quantum aspects of travel, less sure when dealing with the math outside his field, and most inspiring when describing (pp. 98-101) visualization techniques and "*embodied ecstasy*" (ex-stasis, "standing outside" the body; hence embodied ecstasy paradoxically describes the trans-dimensional experience).

Herbert makes no claim to understand the traveling itself, and goes so far as to suggest that even the (unnamed) pioneers who made the first breakthroughs may not have completely understood the process, any more than the inventor of the steam engine understood Classical physics (p. 23). This definitely ties in with what we know about the persons in question.

Unfortunately the six illustrations promised in the table of contents are not included in the galleys — one of them was a "Schematic for a Trans-dimensional Express" which might be worth killing for! — and the publishers claim that Herbert never supplied the illustrations. They refuse to say why they suspended publication of *Alternate Dimensions* and in fact at first denied ever having handled such a title! Moreover Herbert has apparently dropped out of sight; if he hasn't met with foul play, he may have returned permanently to Earth2.

We regret having to sell copies of a flawed book for such an outrageous price; we'd like to publish a mass-market edition affordable by all — but if Harper & Row ever find out what we're doing, we'll need the money for court costs and lawyers' fees! So get it while you can — this is THE indispensable background work for understanding the Conspiracy.

5. Thomsen, Dietrick E.
"A Knowing Universe Seeking to be Known"
(Xerox offprint from *ScienceNews*, Vol. 123, 1983)

Unwittingly demonstrates the resonance between quantum reality theory and the sufism of (for example) "the Greatest Shaykh" Ibn'Arabi, who discusses in his *Bezels of Wisdom* a saying attributed to God by Mohammad (but not in the Koran): "I was a hidden treasure and I wanted (lit. 'loved') to be known; so I created the universe, that I might be known."

5a. We also have a few off-prints (at the same price) of Thomsen's witty "Quanta at Large:101 Things To Do with Schroedinger's Cat" (op. cit,129,1986).

6. DeWitt, Bryce S. & Neill Graham.
The Many Worlds Interpretation of Quantum Mechanics
(Princeton, NJ, 1973)
The standard (and far from "easy"!) work on the Everett/ Wheeler hypothesis — a bible for the early pioneers.

7. Cramer, John G.
"Alternate Universes II"
(Analog, Nov. 1984)
A popularization of the Theory by a prominent physicist — no knowledge of the Conspiracy is detectable. We're selling copies of the Sci-Fi mag itself for $10 each.

8. Greenberg, D.M., ed.
New Techniques & Ideas in Quantum Measurement Theory
(Vol. 480 Annals of the NY Academy of Sciences, 1986)
Contains the valuable if somewhat whimsical article by D. Z. Albers, *"How to take a Photograph of Another Everett World"*. Also the very important *"Macroscopic Quantum Tunneling at Finite Temperatures"* by P. Hanggi (we suspect him of being a Conspiracy member).

9. (Anonymous).
Course Catalogue for 1978-79,Institute of Chaos Studies and Imaginal Yoga
(no address); Xerox of mimeographed flyer, 7pp
An in-house document from the Institute where the first breakthrough was attained (probably in the late winter or early spring of 1979) — therefore, although it makes no overt mention of Travel or the Egg, the *Catalogue* is of prime importance for an understanding of the intellectual and historical background of the event.

According to an unreliable source (see *ESCAPE FROM EARTH PRIME!,*#15 in this list), the Institute was located somewhere in Dutchess County, New York, where the founder and director, Dr. Kamadev Sohrawardi, was employed by IBM in the 1960's, "dropped out" and began investigations into "consciousness physics"; it is also claimed that Sohrawardi was a Bengali of mixed English, Hindu and Moslem origin, descended from an old Sufi family, and initiated into Tantra. All this disagrees with clues in other sources and is perhaps not to be trusted. Other groups take credit for Breakthrough, and Sohrawardi may have been a fraud — but we're convinced that the *Catalogue* is authentic and Sohrawardi's claim the most certain.

At first glance, the *Catalogue* appears an example of late-hippy/early-New-Age pretentiousness. Thus there are courses in "Visions of Color & Light in Sufi Meditation", "Inner Alchemy in Late Taoism", "Metaphysics of the Ismaili 'Assassins'", "Imaginal Yoga & the Psychotoplogy of the Imagination", "Hermetic & Neo-Pagan Studies", (apparently based on Golden Dawn teachings), "Visualization Techniques in Javanese Sorcery", "Stairways to Heaven: Shamanic Trance & the Mapping of Consciousness", "Stirner, Nietzsche & Stone age Economy — An Examination of Non-Authoritarian Hunter/Gatherer Societies", and — interestingly enough! — "Conspiracy Theory".

The "shamanic" course may have been a blind for research in psychotropic drugs, including such exotica asahuasca (yage, harmaline), ibogaine, yohimbine, Telepathine and Viatmin K, as well as the more standard psychedelicatessan of the late 70's.

However, the *Catalogue* also contains amazing courses in frontier science, any combination of which could have provided the key or final puzzle-bit to the Breakthrough: apparently Sohrawardi taught or supervised most of them. Thus "The Universe in a Grain of Sand" promised information on models of brain activity, cybernetically-enhanced feedback, Sheldrake's morphogenetic field theory, Rene' Thom's Catastrophic Theory as applied to consciousness, lucid-dreaming research, John Lilly's work on "altered states" and other mind-related topics. Then in "Strange Attractors & the Mathematics of Chaos", Sohrawardi discussed matters unknown outside of the margins of academia till the mid-80's, and made the astounding prediction that Chaos in the macroscopic world somehow be found to mirror Uncertainty in the microscopic or Quantum World, a truth still unrecognized in "official" scientific circles today. He felt that n-dimensional strange attractors could be used to model the quantum behavior of particles/waves, and that the "so-called collapse of the wave function" could actually be mapped with certain bizarre ramifications of Thom's catastrophic topology. Making references to work by Ilya Prigogine which was still being circulated in private "preprint" or samizdat form at the time, Sohrawardi suggests that "creative chaos" (as opposed to "deterministic" or entropic chaos) provides the link that will unify Relativity, Quantum, Complexity and consciousness itself into a new science.

Finally in his "Advanced Seminar on Many Worlds", he states baldly that the alternative universes predicted by Relativity (Black Hole Theory) are the same as the many worlds predicted by Quantum, *are the same* as fractal dimensions revealed in Chaos! This one-page course description is the closest thing we have to an *explanation* of why travel to other worlds *actually works*. Hence the Catalogue is an indispensable document for the serious student of the Conspiracy.

10. Beckenstein,J.

"Black holes & Entropy"

(Xerox offprint from *Physical Review*,Vol. D7,1973; 28pp)

An early (pre-Breakthrough) speculation with suggestive hints about quantum and chaos-as-entropy — although no knowledge of actual Chaos Theory is demonstrated. This paper was referred to in an in-house memo from the Inst. for Chaos Studies & Imaginal Yoga, believed to have been composed by K. Sohrawardi himself (see #9).

11. Sohrawardi,Dr Kamadev.

"Pholgiston & the Quantum Aether"

(Off print from the *J. of Paranormal Physics*,Vol. XXII, Bombay, 1966)

An early paper by Sohrawardi, flooded with wild speculations about quantum and oriental spirituality, probably dating from the period when he was still working for IBM, but making visits to Millbrook, nearby in Dutchess Co., and participating in the rituals of the League of spiritual discovery under Dr. T Leary, and the psychedelic yoga of Bill Haines' Sri Ram Ashram, which shared Leary's headquarters on a local millionaires estate. The basic insight concerns the identity of Everett/Wheeler's "many worlds" and the "other worlds" of sufism, tantrik Hinduism and Vajrayana Buddhism. At the time, Sohrawardi apparently believed he could "prove" this by reviving the long-dead theories of phlogiston and aether in the light of quantum discoveries! (Phlogiston Theory — based on the thinking of the sufi alchemist Jabir ibn Hayaan — the original Jabir — was propounded seriously in the 18th century to unify heat and light as "one thing".) Totally useless as science, this metaphor nevertheless inspired Sohrawardi's later and genuinely important work on alternate realities.

12. ibid. "Zero Work & Psychic Paleolithism"
East Village Other, **Vol. IV #4**
(Dec. 1968); Xerox reprint, single sheet 11 1/2 x 17
Unfortunately no scientific speculations, but a fascinating glimpse into the *political* background of the inventor of Travel (or rather, one of the inventors). Making reference to French Situationist and Dutch "Provo" ideas which helped spark the "Events" and upheavals of Spring '68 all over Europe and America, Sohrawardi looks forward to a world without "the alienating prison of WORK", restored to the "oneness with Nature of the Old Stone Age" and yet somehow based on "green technology and quantum weirdness."

Wild and wooly as it is, this text nevertheless poses a fascinating scientific question in the light of the author's later accomplishments — a question still unanswered. All the "First Breakthroughs" we know of with any degree of certainty (those in New York, California, and Java — the actual sequence is unclear) without exception entered parallel worlds *without human inhabitants*, virtual forest-worlds. Most science fiction predicated other worlds almost like ours. Populated by "us", with only a few slight differences, worlds "close" to ours. Instead — no people! Why?

Two possible explanations: (1) We cannot enter worlds containing "copies" of ourselves without causing paradox and violating the consistency principle of the "megaverse" — hence only wild (or feral) worlds are open to Travel. (2) Other worlds exist, in a sense, only as probabilities; in order to "become fully real" they must be *observed*. In effect, the parallel universes are *observer-created*, as soon as a traveller "arrives" in one of them. Sohrawardi *wanted* a Paleolithic world of endless forest, plentiful game and gathering, virgin, empty but slightly haunted — therefore, *that's what he got!* Either explanation raises problems in the light of what actually happened; perhaps there is a third, as yet unsuspected.

13. (Anonymous).
Ong's Hat: A Color Brochure of the Institute of Chaos Studies **(photocopy of the original color brochure)**
Note — This is one of the RARE pamphlets from this series that I have been able to procure. It is included in the next chapter of this book. — Joseph Matheny

This bizarre document, disguised as a brochure for a New Age health retreat, reveals some interesting information about the activities of Sohrawardi group or a closely-associated group. A fairly accurate description of the Egg is provided, as well as a believable account of the first (or one of the first) Breakthroughs. However, everything else in the pamphlet is sheer disinformation. The New Jersey Pine Barrens were never a center of alternate-worlds research, and all the names in the text are false. A non-existent address is included. Nevertheless, highly valuable for background.

14. "Sven Saxon".
The Stone Age Survivalist
(Loompanics, UnLtd., Port Townsend, WA 1985), Pb

"Imagine yourself suddenly plunked down buck-naked in the middle of a large dark forest with no resources except your mind," says the preface. *"What would you do?"*

What indeed? and who could possibly care? — except a trans-dimensional Traveller! Loompanics specializes in books on disappearances and survival involving a good deal of escapist fantasy — but as we know, this situation is all too real for the Visitor to Other Worlds.

Part I: Flint-knapping, an excellent illustrated handbook of Paleolithic tool-production; II Zero-tech hunting and trapping; III, Gathering (incl. a materia medica); IV, Shelter; V, Primitive warfare; VI, Man & Dog: trans-species symbiosis; VII, Cold weather survival; VIII, Culture ("Sven" recommends memorizing a lot of songs, poems and stories — and ends by saying "*Memorize this book* — cause you can't take it with you". Where is "Mr. Saxon" now, we wonder?).

15. Balcombe, Harold S.
Escape From Earth Prime!
(Foursquare Press, Denver, Colo., 1986), Pb

This — unfortunately! — is the book that blew the lid off the Conspiracy for the first time. We say "unfortunately" because ESCAPE!, to all appearances, is a piece of unmitigated paranoid pulp tripe. Written in breathless ungrammatical subFortean prose, unfootnoted and nakedly sensationalistic, the book sank without trace, ignored even by the kook-conspiracy fringe; we were able to buy out unsold stock from the vanity press which published it, just before they went out of business and stopped answering their mail.

Balcombe (whom we've been unable to trace and who may have "vanished"), is the author of one other book we've seen — but are not offering for sale — called *Drug Lords from the Hollow Earth* (1984) in which he claims that the CIA obtained LSD and cocaine from Dero-flying-saucer-nazis from beneath Antarctica. So much for his credentials. How he got hold of even a bit of the authentic Other Worlds story is a miracle.

According to Balcombe, the first breakthrough was due not solely to K. Soharawardi — despite his importance as a theoretician — but also a "sinister webwork of cultists, anarchists, commies, fanatical hippies and renegade traitor scientists who made fortunes in the drug trade" (p. 3). Balcombe promises to name names, and out of the welter of rant and slather, some hard facts about the pioneers actually emerge.

Funding (and some research) emanated in the 70's from a "chaos cabal" of early Silicon Valley hackers interested in complex dynamical systems, randomicity, and chance, and — gambling! — as well as a shadowy group of "drug lords" (Balcombe's favorite term of abuse), with connections to certain founders of the Discordian Illuminati. Money was channeled through a cult called the Moorish Orthodox Church, a loose knit confederation of jazz musicians, oldtime hipsters, white "sufis" and black moslems, bikers and street dealers (see "A Heresologist's Guide to Brooklyn", #24 in this list) who came into contact with Sohrawardi in Millbrook in the mid-60's.

Sohrawardi was a naive idealist and somewhat careless about his associations. He received clandestine support from people who were in turn connected to certain Intelligence circles with an interest in psychedelic and fringe mind-science. According to Balcombe this was *not* the CIA (MK-ULTRA) but an unofficial offshoot of several groups with Masonic connections! The Conspiracy was penetrated almost from the start, but was actually *encouraged* in the hope of gleaning useful information about parallel worlds, or at least about the "mental conditioning techniques" developed as part of the basic research.

By the mid-70's, Sohrawardi and his various cohorts and connections (now loosely referred to as "the Garden of Forked Paths" or GFP) had become aware of the Intelligence circles (now loosely grouped as "Probability Control Force" or PCF) and had in turn planted double-agents, and gone further underground. In 1978 or 79 an actual device for trans-dimensional Travel, the "Egg" (also called the Cocoon or the Cucurbit, which means both *gourd* and *alchemical flask*) was developed in deepest secrecy, probably at Sohrawardi's institute in Upstate New York, certainly not at a branch lab supposedly hidden away in the NJ Pine Barrens near the long-vanished village of Ong's Hat (see #13 in this list), since no such lab ever existed, nor does it exist now, despite what some fools think.

The PCF were unable to obtain an Egg for several years and did not succeed in Breakthrough until (Balcombe believes) 1982. The California groups, however, began Egg production and broke through (into "BigSur2") in early 1980 (again, Balcombe's chronology). (Balcombe clearly knows nothing of the situation in Java.)

It remains unclear whether the East Coast and West Coast groups both entered the same alternate world, or two *different* but similar worlds. Communication between the two outposts has so far proved impossible because, as it happens, the Egg will not transport *non-sentient matter*. Travellers arrive Over There birth — naked in a Stone Age world — no airplanes, no radio, no clothes...no fire and no tools! Only the Egg, like a diamond Faberge Easter gift designed by Dali, alone in the midst of "Nature naturing". Balcombe includes a dim out-of-focus photo of an Egg, and claims that the machine is part computer but also partly — living crystal, like virus or DNA, and also partly "naked quantumstuff".

Eggs are costly to produce, so the early pioneers had to return after each sortie and forego permanent settlement on E2 until a cheaper mode of transport could be discovered. However, emigration via the Egg proved possible when the "tantrik" or "double-yolk" effect was discovered: two people (any combination of age, gender, etc.) can Travel by Egg while *making love*, especially if one of the pair has already done the trip a few times and "knows the way" without elaborate visualization techniques and so forth. Balcombe has a field day with this juicy information and spends an entire chapter (VIII) detailing the "perversions" in use for this purpose. Talent for Travel ranges from brilliant to zero — probably no more than 15% of humanity can make it, although the less — talented and even children can be "translated" — and extensive training methods have somewhat improved the odds. California2 now contains about 1000 emigrants scattered along the coast, and the eastern settlements add up to 500 or 600. A few children have been born "over there" — some can Travel, some can't, although the talented percentage seems greater than among the general population of Earth-prime.

And being "stuck" on E2 is no grave punishment in any case!, unless you object to the Garden of Eden and the "original leisure society" of the Paleolithic flintknappers.

Balcombe claims that the PCF was severely disappointed by the sentience "law" of Travel, since they had hoped to use the parallel worlds as a weapons — delivery system! Nevertheless they continued to experiment, hoping for a more "mechanistic" technique; meanwhile they devote their efforts to (a) suppressing all information leaks, (b) plotting against the independent GFP and infiltrating the E2 settlements, (c) attempting to open new worlds where technology might be possible. They are however handicapped by a shortage of talent: the kind of person who can Travel is not usually the kind of person who sympathizes with the "patriotic discipline of the PCF" and rogue Masonic groups, but some of these end up defecting and "doubling", and anyway most of them are much too *weird* for the taste of the rigidly reactionary inner core of PCF leadership, who wonder (as does Balcombe) whether these agents are "any better than the scum they're spying on?"

More worlds have been discovered — E3 and E4 are mentioned in *ESCAPE!* (and we know that E5 was opened in 1988) — but all of these are "empty" forest worlds apparently almost identical with E2.

In summary, Balcombe's style is execrable and attitude repulsive, but his book remains the most accurate overview of the Conspiracy to date. If you're only going to order one item from us, this is it.

16. (Anonymous)
"Bionic Travel: An Orgonomic Theory of the Megaverse"
(Xerox of unpubl. typescript headed "Top Secret Q Eyes Only"; 27pp)
If this paper emanates from PCF sources, as we believe, it indicates the poor quality of original research carried out by the enemies of Sohrawardi and the GFP, and may explain the PCF's relative lack of progress in the field (especially considering their much larger budget!). The author attempts to revive W. Reich's

Orgone Theory, with "bions" as "life-force particles" and some sort of orgone accumulator (Reich's "box") as a possible substitute for the Egg. An unhealthy interest is shown in "harnessing the force of *Deadly Orgone*" as a weapon for use on other worlds. References are also made to Aliester Crowley's "sex magick techniques" of the Ordo Templi Orientis even speculations on human *sacrifice* as a possible source of "transdimensional energy". A morbid and crackpot document, devoid of all scientific value (in our opinion) but affording a fascinating insight into PCF mentality and method.

17. Corbin, Henry.
Creative Imagination in the Sufism of Ibn'Arabi
(trans. by R. Mannheim; Princeton, NJ,1969)
One of the few books mentioned by title in the Catalogue of the Inst. of Chaos Studies & Imaginal Yoga (see #9 in this list). The *"mundus imaginalis"*, also called the World of Archetypes or the "Isthmus" (Arabic, barzakh), lies in-between the World of the Divine and the material World of Creation. It actually consists of "many worlds", including two "emerald cities" called Jabulsa and Jabulqa (very intriguing considering the situation on Java2!). The great 14th-century Hispano-Moorish sufi Ibn'Arabi developed a metaphysics of the "Creative Imagination" by which the adept could achieve spiritual progress via direct contemplation of the archetypes, including the domains of djinn, spirits and angels. Ibn'Arabi also speaks of seven alternate Earths created by Allah, each with its own Mecca and Kaaba! Some parallel-universe theorists believe that Travel without any tech (even the Egg) may be possible, claiming that certain mystics have already accomplished it. If so, then Ibn'Arabi must have been one of them.

18. Gleick, James.
CHAOS: Making a New Science
(Viking Penguin, NY, 1987) 254pp
The first and still the most complete introduction to chaos — required reading — BUT with certain caveats. First: Gleick has

no philosophical or poetic depth; he actually begins the book with a quote from John Updike! No mention of chaos mythology or oriental sources. No mention of certain non-American chaos scientists such as Rene Thom and Ilya Prigogine! Instead, alongside the admittedly useful info, one gets a subtle indoctrination in "deterministic chaos", by which we mean the tendency to look on chaos as a weapon to *fight chaos*, to "save" Classical physics Q and learn to predict the Stock Market! (As opposed to what we call the "quantum chaos" of Sohrawardi and his allies, which looks on chaos as a creative and negentropic source, the cornucopia of evolution and awareness.) Warning: we suspect Gleick of being a PCF agent who has embedded his text with subtle disinformation meant to distract the chaos science community from any interest in "other worlds".

19. Pak Hardjanto.
"Apparent Collapse of the Wave Function as an n Dimensional Catastrophe"
(trans. by "N.N.S." in Collected Papers of the SE Asian Soc. for Advanced Research, Vol. XXIX, 1980), 47pp, xerox of offprint
An early paper by the little-known scientific director of the Javanese "Travel Cult" which succeeded in breakthrough, possibly in the year this essay was published or shortly thereafter. Hardjanto is known to have been in touch with Sohrawardi since the 60's; no doubt they shared all information, but each kept the other secret from their respective organizations. The pioneers of Java2 became known to the GFP and PCF only around 1984 or 85.

This article, the only scientific work we possess by Hardjanto, shows him to be a theoretician equal or even superior to Sohrawardi himself — and if Hardjanto is also the anonymous author of the following item, as we believe, then he appears a formidable "metaphysicist" as well!

"Apparent Collapse", while certainly not a blueprint for Egg construction, nevertheless constitutes one of the few bits of "hard" science published openly on our Subject. Unfortunately, its theorems and diagrams are doubtless comprehensible only to a handful of experts. The topological drawings literally boggle the mind, especially one entitled "*Hypercube Undergoing 'Collapse' Into 5 — Space Vortex*"!

20. (Unsigned, probably by Pak Hardjanto).
A Vision of Hurqalya
(trans.by K. K. Sardono; Incunabula Press, 1988), Pb, 46pp

The Indonesian original of this text appeared as a pamphlet in Yogjakarta (E.Java) in 1982. We ourselves at Incunabula commissioned the translation and have published this handsome edition, including all the illustrations from the original, at our own expense.

If one knew nothing about the Conspiracy or Many-Worlds Theory, A Vision would seem at first to be a mystical tract by an adherent of *kebatinan*, the heterodox sufi influenced freeform esoteric/syncretistic complex of sects which has come to be influential in GFP circles, inasmuch as the idea of "spiritual master" (guru, murshed) has been replaced by "teacher" *(pamong)*; some kebatinan sects utilize spontaneous non-hierarchical organizational structures.

However, in the light of our knowledge of the material existence of other worlds, Vision takes on a whole new dimension Q as a literal description of what Hardjanto and his fellow pioneers found on Java2.

They discovered another uninhabited world — but with one huge difference. The author of Vision steps out of his "alchemical Egg" into a vast and ancient abandoned City! He calls it Hurqalya (after a traditional sufi name for the Other World or *alam-e-mithal*). He senses his total aloneness — feels that the City's builders have long since moved on *elsewhere* — and yet that they still somehow somewhere exist.

The author compares Hurqalya to the ancient ruined city of Borobadur in E. Java, but notices immediately that there are no statues or images — all the decoration is abstract and severe — but "neither Islamic nor Buddhist nor Hindu nor Christian nor any style I ever saw". The "palaces" of Hurqalya are grand, cyclopean, almost monolithic — far from "heavy" in atmosphere, despite the black basalt from which they seem to have been carved. For the City is cut through by water...it is in fact a water — city in the style of the Royal Enclave of Yogjakarta (now so sadly derelict) — but incomparably bigger. Canals, aqueducts, rivers and channels crisscross and meander through the City; flowing originally from quiescent volcanic mountains looming green in the West. Water flows down through the City which is built on a steep slope gradually curving into a basin and down to the placid Eastern Sea, where a hundred channels flow dark and clear into the green salt ocean.

Despite the air of ruin — huge trees have grown through buildings, splitting them open — mosses, ferns and orchids coat the crumbling walls with viridescence, hosting parrots, lizards, butterflies — despite this desolation, most of the waterworks still flow: canal-locks broken open centuries ago allow cascades, leaks, spills and waterfalls in unexpected places, so that the City is wrapped in a tapestry of water sounds and songbird voices. Most amazingly, the water flows at different levels simultaneously, so that aqueducts cross over canals which in turn flow above sunken streams which drip into wells, underground cisterns and mysterious sewers in a bewildering complex of levels, pipes, conduits and irrigated garden terraces which resemble (to judge by the author's sketches) a dreamscape of Escher or Piranesi. Viewed from above, the City would be mapped as an arabesque 3PD spiderweb (with waterbridges aboveground, streams at ground level and also underground) fanning out to fill the area of the basin, thence into the harbor with its huge cracked basalt block docks.

The slope on which the City is built is irregularly terraced in ancient SE Asian style — as many staircases as streets thread their way up and down, laid out seemingly at random, following land contours rather than grid logic, adding to the architectural complexity of the layer of waterways with a maze of vine encrusted overpasses, arched bridges, spiraling ramps, crooked alleyways, cracked hidden steps debouching on broad esplanades, avenues, parks gone to seed, pavilions, balconies, apartments, jungle choked palazzos, echoing gloomy "temples" whose divinities, if any, seem to have left no forwarding address ... all empty, all utterly abandoned. And nowhere is there any human debris — no broken tools, bones or midden heaps, no evidence of actual habitation — as if the ancient builders of the City picked up and took everything with them when they departed — "perhaps to one of the other Seven Worlds of the alam-e-mithal" — in other words, to a "higher dimension.

Thus ends the *Vision of Hurqalya* — raising more questions than it answers! There is no doubt that it describes exactly what was discovered in Java2 in 1980 or 81. But if the "observer-created" theory of other-worlds Travel is true, "Hurqalya" represents the "imaginal imprint" of what Hardjanto (or whoever) *expected* to find. Yet again, if that theory is false ... *who built Hurqalya?* One current explanation (arising from time distortion theorems which have so far remained unsolvable) suggests that the Builders "moved" in prehistoric times to Earth -prime and became the distant ancestors of the Javanese ("Java Man"). Another guess: the Builders have indeed moved on to a "distant" alternate universe, and eventually *we may find them.*

A small settlement now exists in Hurqalya. Once the American groups heard of the City's existence, members of both the GFP and PFC were able to visualize it and Travel to it *from America* (the Javanese can do the same from Java-prime to America2). Since 1985 all three groups have expanded most of their exploratory effort on "opening up" new worlds in the Java series. Apparently Indonesian sorcerers and trance adepts are *very* good at this, and we believe they have reached Java7 — without, however, finding replications of the City or any trace of the Builders — only more empty forest.

21. Von Bitter Rucker, Dr R.
"The Cat Was Alive, But Looked Scared As Hell": Some Unexpected Properties of Cellular Automata in the Light of the Everett-Wheeler Hypothesis"
(Complex Dynamical Systems Newsletter no. 8, 1989), offprint

Who is this man and what does he know? No other serious mathematician has so far made any connection between cellular automata and the Many Worlds. Tongue-in-cheek (?), the author suggests that Schroedinger's poor cat might be *both* alive *and* dead, even after the box is opened, IF parallel universes are "stacked" in some arcane manner which he claims to be able to demonstrate with a piece of software he has hacked and is selling for an outrageous sum; we have also seen an ad for this program in a magazine called *MONDO 2000*, published in Berkeley and devoted to "reality hacking". We'd love to know what certain members of the Conspiracy would make of this bizarre concept!

22. Kennedy, Alison.
"Psychotropic Drugs in 'Shared-World'& Lucid Dreaming Experiments"
(Psychedelic Monographs & Essays, Vol. XIV, no. 2, 1981, offprint)
This writer appears to have inside information. The notion of a drug-induced hallucination so powerful it can be shared by many (in a proper "blind" experiment) and can actually *come into existence*, into material reality; the idea that drug-enhanced lucid dreaming can be used to discover objective information from "other ontological levels of being"; and finally the "prediction" that "a combination of these methods utilizing computer aided biofeedback monitoring devices" will actually make it possible to "visit 'other' worlds in 'inner' space" (which suggests that the author adheres to the "observer-created" theory of parallel universes) — all this leads us to believe that the author is probably a member of one of the California Travel Cults — as well as an expert *bruja*!

23. (Anonymous).
A Collection of Cult Pamphlets, Flyers, Ephemera & Curiosa from the Library of a Traveler
(Loose-leaf portfolio of photocopied originals) sold by lot
The unknown compiler of this Collection (whom for convenience we'll call "X") left it behind when he "vanished",

whence it came into our possession. We know something of the compiler's career from an untitled document written by him and found with the Collection, which we call *The Poetic Journal of a Traveller* (#24 in this list), as well as a pamphlet believed to be by the same author, *Folklore of the Other Worlds* (#25). *(The Ong's Hat Color Brochure* was also discovered in the same cache, and is sold by us as #13.)

The Collection contains the following items:

1) *A History & Catechism of the Moorish Orthodox Church*, which traces the origins of the sect to early (1913) American Black Islam, the "Wandering Bishops", the Beats of the 50s and the psychedelic churches movement of the 60s — deliberately vague about the 70s and 80s however.

2) *The World Congress of Free Religions*, a brochure — manifesto arguing for a "fourth way", a non-authoritarian spiritual movement in opposition to mainstream, fundamentalist and New Age religion. The WCFR is said to include various sects of Discordians, SubGeniuses, Coptic Orthodox People of the Herb, gay ("faery") neo-pagans, Magical Judaism, the Egyptian Church of New Zealand, Kaos Kabal of London, Libertarian Congregationalists, etc. Q and the Moorish Orthodox Church. Several of these sects are implicated in the Conspiracy, but no overt mention of the Travel Cults is made here.

3) *Spiritual Materialism*, by "the New Catholic Church of the Pantarchy, Hochkapel von SS Max und Marx", a truly weird flyer dedicated to "Saints" Max Stirner and Karl Marx, representing a group claiming foundation by the 19th century Individualist Stephen Pearl Andrews, but more likely begun in the 1980s as a Travel Cult. Uses Nietzsche to contend that material reality itself constitutes a (or the) spiritual value and the principle of Infinity "which is expressed in the existence of many worlds. " It argues for a utopia based on "individual-ism, telepathic socialism, free love, high tech, Stone Age wilderness and quantum weirdness"! No address is given, needless to say.

4) *The Sacred Jihad of Our Lady of Chaos*, this otherwise untraceable group calls for "resistance to all attempts to control probability." It quotes Foucault and Baudrillard on the subject of "disappearance", then suggests that "to vanish without having to

kill yourself may be the ultimate revolutionary act ... The monolith of Consensus Reality is riddled with quantum-chaos cracks ... Viral attack on all fronts! Victory to Chaos in every world!"

5) *The Temple of Antinous*, a Travel Cult of neo-pagans devoted to Eros and Ganymede. (Warning: this leaflet contains some just-barely-legal graphic material.) "Wistfully we wonder if the boygod can manifest only in some other world than this dreary puritanical polluted boobocracy — then, gleefully, we suddenly recall: *there ARE other worlds!*"

6) A Collage, presumably made by X himself, consisting of a "mandala" constructed from cut-outs of Strange Attractors and various Catastrophic topologies interwoven with photos of young women clipped from Italian fashion magazines. Eroticizing the mathematical imagery no doubt helps one to remember and visualize it while operating the Egg.

24. (Anonymous).
Poetic Journal of a Traveller; or, A Heresologist's Guide to Brooklyn
(Incunabula Press, pamphlet, Believed to be by "X", the compiler of the Collection, & transcribed by us from manuscript.)
Apparently X began this MS with the intention of detailing his experiences with a Travel Cult and eventual "translation" to the various alternate-world settlements, but unfortunately abandoned the project early on, possibly due to PCF interference.

It begins with a summary account of X's spiritual quest, largely among the stranger sects of his native Brooklyn: Santeria in Coney Island, Cabala in Williamsburg, sufis on Atlantica Avenue, etc. He is disappointed or turned away (and even mugged on one occasion). He becomes friendly with a Cuban woman of mixed Spanish, black, amerindian and Chinese ancestry who runs a botanica (magical supplies and herbs). When he asks her about "other worlds", she is evasive but promises to introduce him to someone who knows more about such matters.

She orders her grand-daughter, a 14-year-old named Teofila *(see the graphic novel, page 160 of this book for a rendition of*

Teofila by artist Tony Talbert), to escort X through the "rough neighborhoods" to the old man's shop. The girl is wearing a t-shirt that says "Hyperborean Skateboarding Association", and indeed travels by skateboard, "gliding on ahead of me like Hermes the Psychopomp." X is clearly attracted to Teofila and becomes embarrassedly tongue-tied and awkward.

The old man, called "the Shaykh", who claims to be Sudanese but speaks "pure Alabaman", runs a junk shop and wears a battered old Shriners fez. His attitude toward X is severe at first, but X is enchanted by his rather disjointed rambling and ranting — which reveal a surprisingly wide if erratic reading in Persian poetry, the Bible, Meister Eckhardt, William Blake, Yoruba mythology and quantum mechanics. Leaving the girl in the shop, the old man takes X into his back office, "crowded with wildly eclectic junk, naive paintings, cheap orientalismo, HooDoo candles, jars of flower petals, and an ornate potbellied stove, stoked up to cherryred, suffusing waves of drowsy warmth."

The Shaykh intimidates X into sharing a big pipe of hashish mixed with amber and mescaline, then launches into a stream-of-consciousness attack on "Babylon, the Imperium, the Con, the Big Lie that there's nowhere to go and nothing to buy except their fifth-rate imitations of life, their bullshit pie-in-the-sky religions, cold cults, cold cuts of self-mutilation I call 'em, and woe to Jerusalem!" X, now "stoned to the gills", falls under the Shaykh's spell and bursts into tears. At once the old man unbends, serves X a cup of tea "sweetblack as Jamaica run and scented with cardamon", and begins to drop broad hints about "a way out, not to some gnostic-never-land with the body *gone* like a fart in a sandstorm, no brother, for the Unseen World is not just of the spirit but also the flesh Q Jabulsa and Jabulqa, Hyperborea, Hurqalya Q they're as real as Brooklyn but a *damn* sight prettier!"

Late afternoon; X must return home before dark, and prepare to take leave of the Shaykh Q who gives him a few pamphlets and invites him to return. To X's surprise, Teofila is still waiting outside the shop, and offers to escort him to the subway. The girl is now in a friendlier mood and X less nervous. They strike up a conversation, X asking about Hyperborea and Teofila answering,

"Yeah, I know where it is — I've *been* there."

The main narrative ends here, but we have added some other poetic fragments included with the original MS, despite the fact that they might offend some readers, in light of the importance of the "tantrik technique" of other-world Travel. (And let us remind you that a statement of age must be included with every order from Incunabula Inc.). These rather pornographic fragments suggest that X, too shy to attempt anything himself, was in fact seduced by Teofila, and that his subsequent "training" for Egg-navigation consisted of numerous "practice sessions for double-"yolking" with a very enthusiastic young tutor.

We believe that X subsequently made an extended visit to America2 and Java2, that he returned to Earth-prime on some Intelligence or sabotage mission for the GFP, that he composed a paper on *Folklore of the Other Worlds* (see #25), that he and Teofila somehow came to the attention of PCF agents in New York, aborted their mission and returned to Java2, where they presumably now reside.

25. (Anonymous).
Folklore of the Other Worlds
(Incunabula Press, pamphlet, By the same author as #24, transcribed by us from manuscript.)
Our anonymous Traveller from Brooklyn appears to have composed this little treatise after his first extended stay in E2. It deals with tales of Travellers and inhabitants of the other-world settlements, pioneers' experiences and the like. Of great interest is the claim that ESP and other paranormal abilities increase in the parallel universes, that the effect is magnified by passing through the series of discovered "levels", and that a small band of psychic researchers has therefore settled on Java7, the present frontier world. The "temple" of Hurqalya (or whatever these vast buildings may have been) are used for sessions of meditation, martial arts and psychic experimentation. X claims that telepathy is now accepted as fact "over there," with strong evidence for telekinesis and perhaps even Egg-less Travel.

Also intriguing are various accounts of "spirits" seen or sensed around the settlements, were-animals supposedly glimpsed on higher levels, and legends which have arisen concerning the lost Builders of Hurqalya. Something of a cult has grown up around these hypothetical creatures who (it is said) are "moving toward us even as we move toward them, through the dimensions, through Time — perhaps backwards through Time"!

X points out that this legend strikes an eerie resonance with "complex conjugate wave theory" in quantum mechanics, which hypothesizes that the "present" (the Megaverse "now") is the result of the meeting of two infinite quantum probability waves, one moving from past to future, the other moving from future to past — that space/time is an interference effect of these two waves — and that the many worlds are bubbles on this shoreline!

26. Eliade, Mircea.
Shamanism: Archaic Techniques of Ecstasy
(Univ. of Chicago Press), Pb

This "bible" of the modern neo-shamanic movement also served as a metaphorical scripture for the pioneers of interdimensional consciousness physics and alternate-world explorers. Not only does it contain innumerable practical hints for the Traveller, as well as a spiritual ambience conducive to the proper state of mind for Travel — it is also believed that Eliade's mythic material on the prototypal Stone Age shamans who could *physically and actually* visit other worlds, offers strong evidence for the possibility of Egg-less Travel — which however so far remains in the realm of "folklore", speculation and rumor.

27. Lorde, John.
Maze of Treason
(Red Knight Books, Wildwood,NJ,1988), Pb, 204 pp

You may remember that after the Patty Hearst kidnapping it was discovered that a cheap pornographic thriller, published *before* the event, seemed to foretell every detail of the story. Jungian synchronicity? Or did the Symbioses Liberation Army read that book and decide to act it out? It remains a mystery.

Maze of Treason is also a pornographic thriller, complete with tawdry 4-color cover, sloppy printing on acidulous pulp, and horrendous style. It's marketed as Science Fiction, however. And there is no mystery about the author's inside knowledge. "John Lorde" not only knows about the Conspiracy, he's obviously been there. This book is probably a *roman a clef*, as it appears to contain distorted portraits of Sohrawardi and Harjanto (depicted as Fu-Manchu-type villains) as well as several actual agents of both the GFP and PCF — and even a character apparently based on the real-life "X", author of several titles in our list (#s 24 & 25).

The hero, Jack Masters, is an agent of an unnamed spyforce of American patriots who jokingly call themselves the Quantum Police. Their mission is to regain control of the alternate worlds for "the forces of reason and order" and "make trouble for agents of chaos in every known universe." The Q-Cops' secret underground HDQ contains a number of Eggs granting access to hidden bases on the other worlds, including "the Other America" and "the Other Indonesia".

Jack Masters is investigating the activities of a Chaote named Ripley Taylor, a "child-molester and black magician" who runs a Travel Cult out of a comic book store in a "racially mixed neighborhood" of New York. The Cops hope to catch Taylor with his "juvenile delinquent girlfriend", blackmail him and turn him into a double agent.

The hero now becomes involved with Amanita, a beautiful woman performance artist from the Lower East Side who seems to know a lot about Taylor and the Travel Cult, but also seems quite attracted to the virile Jack Masters. At first he suspects her of duplicity, but soon decides he needs to "convert" her by making her "fall for me, and fall hard. " Jack's problem is that his own "talent" will not suffice for solo Travelling, and in fact he has never managed to "get across" — since the Cops do not practice Tantrik techniques! He suspects her of being an "Other-Worlder" and hopes she can convey him thence via the "infamous 'double -yolk' method."

Meanwhile Taylor has laughed off the blackmail attempt, burned down the comic shop and escaped "into the fourth dimension — or maybe the fifth." Masters heats up his affair with the artist Amanita, and finally convinces her to "translate" him — after three chapters of unininterrupted porno depicting the pair in many little-known ritual practices, so to speak. (The author rises above his own mediocrity here, and attains something like "purple pulp", an inspired gush of horny prose, especially in the oral-genital area.) Masters now rises to the occasion for yet a fourth chapter in which a "government-issue Egg" becomes the setting for a "yab-yum ceremony of searing obscenity. "

Immediately upon arrival in "Si Fan" (the author's name for Hurqalya), Amanita betrays our hero and turns him over naked to one of the tribes of "chaos-shamans who inhabit these Lemur Ian ruins". At this point *Maze* begins to add to our knowledge of the real-life situation by depicting more-or-less accurately the state of affairs and mode of life in present-day Hurqalya — at least, as seen through the eyes of a paranoid right-wing spy.

The thousand or so inhabitants have made few changes in Hurqalya, preferring a life of "primitive sloth" and minimal meddling with Nature. Sex, hallucinogenic mushrooms and song improvisation contests comprise the nightlife, with days devoted to the serious business of "sorcery, skinny-dipping, flint knapping and maybe a couple of hours of desultory fishing or berry picking." There is no social order. "People with bones in their noses sitting around arguing about Black Hole Theory or recipes for marsupial stew — lazy smoke from a few clan campfires rising through the hazy bluegold afternoon — people masturbating in trees — bees snouting into orchids — signal drum in the distance — Amanita singing an old song by the Inkspots I remember from my childhood..."

Masters — or rather the author — claims to be disgusted by all this "anarchist punk hippy immorality — all this jungle love!" — but his ambivalence is revealed in his continued desire for Amanita, and the ease with which he falls into his own curmudgeonly version of *dolce far niente* in "Si Fan".

We won't give away the rest of the plot, not because it's so great, but because it's largely irrelevant (Taylor flees to distant dimensions, Masters gets Girl and returns to Earth-prime in triumph, etc., etc.) — the book's true value lies in these pictures of daily life in Hurqalya. Sadly, *Maze of Treason* is still our only source for such material.

The Conspiracy to deny the world all knowledge of the Many Worlds is maintained by both the forces active in the parallel universes — the GFP and PCF both have their reasons for secrecy, evasion, lies, disinformation, distortion and even violence. *Maze of Treason* is not our only source for claiming that people have lost their lives as a result of getting too deeply involved in all this. But we at INCUNABULA believe that truth will out, because it must. To stand in the way of it is more dangerous than letting it loose. Freedom of information is our only protection — we will tell all, despite all scorn or threat, and trust that our "going public" will protect us from the outrage of certain private interests — if not from the laughter of the ignorant!

Remember: parallel worlds exist. They have *already been reached*. A vast cover-up denies YOU all knowledge. Only INCUNABULA can enlighten you, because only INCUNABULA dares.

Thank You,
Emory Cranston, Prop.

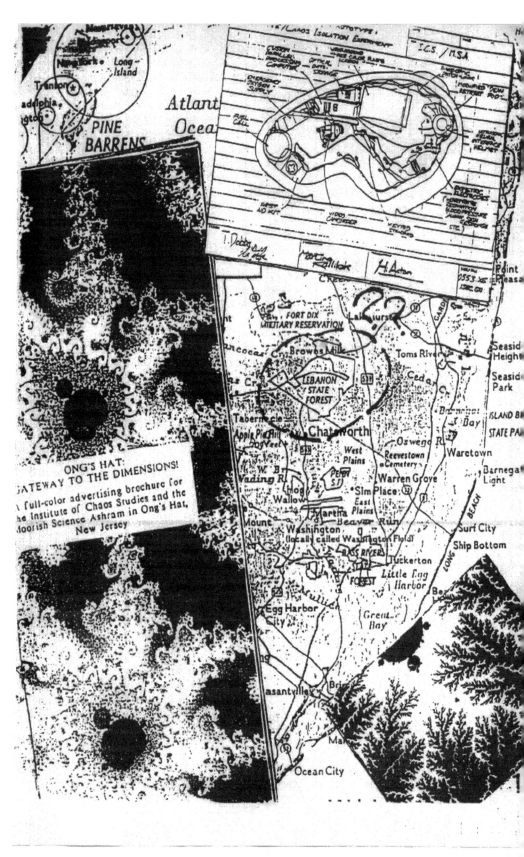

ONG'S HAT:
GATEWAY TO THE DIMENSIONS!

A full-color advertising brochure for the Institute of Chaos Studies and the Moorish Science Ashram in Ong's Hat, New Jersey

ONG'S HAT: GATEWAY TO THE DIMENSIONS!

A full color brochure for the Institute of Chaos Studies and the Moorish Science Ashram in Ong's Hat, New Jersey.

Introductions

You would not be reading this brochure if you had not already penetrated half-way to the ICS. You have been searching for us without knowing it, following oblique references in crudely Xeroxed marginal "samisdat" publications, crackpot mystical pamphlets, mailorder courses in "Kaos Magick" — a paper trail and a coded series of rumors spread at street level through circles involved in the illicit distribution of certain controlled substances and the propagation of certain acts of insurrection against the Planetary Work Machine and the Consensus Reality — or perhaps through various obscure mimeographed technical papers on the edges of "chaos science" — through pirate computer networks — or even through pure synchronicity and the pursuit of dreams.

In any case we know something about you, your interests, deeds and desires, works and days — and we know your address.

Otherwise...you would not be reading this brochure.

Background

During the 1970s and '80s, "chaos" began to emerge as a new scientific paradigm, on a level of importance with Relativity and Quantum Mechanics. It was born out of the mixing of many different sciences — weather prediction, Catastrophe Theory, fractal geometry, and the rapid development of computer graphics capable of plunging into the depths of fractals and "strange attractors; hydraulics and fluid turbulence, evolutionary biology, mind/brain studies and psychopharmacology also played major roles in forming the new paradigm."

The slogan "order out of chaos" summed up the gist of this science, whether it studied the weird fractional-dimensional shapes underlying swirls of cigarette smoke or the distribution of colors in marbled paper-or else dealt with "harder" matters such as heart fibrillation, particle beams or population vectors.

However, by the late '80s it began to appear as if this "chaos movement" had split apart into two opposite and hostile world-views, one placing emphasis on chaos itself, the other on *order*.

According to the latter sect — the Determinists — chaos was the enemy, randomness a force to be overcome or denied. They experienced the new science as a final vindication of Classical Newtonian physics, and as a weapon to be used *against* chaos, a tool to map and predict reality itself. For them, chaos was death and disorder, entropy and waste.

The opposing faction however experienced chaos as something benevolent, the necessary matrix out of which arises spontaneously an infinity of variegated forms — a pleroma rather than an abyss — a principle of continual creation, unstructured, fecund, beautiful, spirit of wildness. These scientists saw chaos theory as vindication of Quantum indeterminacy and Godel's Proof, promise of an open-ended universe, Cantorian infinities of potential...chaos as *health*.

Easy to predict which of these two schools of thought would receive vast funding and support from governments, multinationals and intelligence agencies. By the end of the decade, "Quantum/Chaos" had been forced underground, virtually censored by prestigious scientific journals — which published only papers by Determinists.

The dissidents were reduced to the level of the *margin* — and there they found themselves part of yet another branch of the paradigm, the underground of cultural chaos — the "magicians" — and of political chaos-extremist anti-authoritarian "mutants".

Unlike Relativity, which deals with the Macrocosm of outer space, and Quantum, which deals with the Microcosm of particle physics, chaos science takes place largely within the Mesosphere — the world as we experience it in "everyday life", from dripping faucets to banners flapping in the autumn breezes. Precisely for this reason useful experimental work in chaos can be carried on without the hideous expense of cyclotrons and orbital observatories.

So even when the leading theoreticians of Quantum/Chaos began to be fired from university and corporate positions, they were still able to pursue certain goals. Even when they began to suffer political pressures as well, and sought refuge and space among the mutants and marginals, still they perservered. By a paradox of history, their poverty and obscurity forced them to narrow the scope of their research to precisely those areas which would ultimately produce concrete results — pure math, and the mind — simply because these areas were relatively inexpensive.

Up until the crash of '87, the "alternative network" amounted to little more than a nebulous weave of pen-pals and computer enthusiasts, Whole Earth nostalgists, futurologists, anarchists, food cranks, neo-pagans and cultists, self-publishing punk poets, armchair schizophrenics, survivalists and mail artists. The Crash however opened vast but hard-to-see cracks in the social and economic control structures of America. Gradually the marginals and mutants began to fill up those fissures with the wegs of their own networking. Bit by bit they created a genuine black economy, as well as a shifting insubstantial "autonomous zone", impossible to map but real enough in its various manifestations.

The orphaned scientists of Q/C theory fell into this invisible anti-empire like a catalyst — or perhaps it was the other way around. In either case, something crystallized. To explain the precipitation of this jewel, we must move on to the specific cases, people and stories.

History

The Moorish Orthodox Church of America is an offshoot of the Moorish Science Temple, the New World's first Islamic heretical sect, founded by a black circus magician named Noble Drew Ali in Newark, New Jersey in 1913. In the 1950s some white jazz musicians and poets who held "passports" in the M.S.T. founded the Moorish Orthodox Church, which also traced its spiritual ancestry to various "Wandering Bishops" loosely affiliated with the Old Catholic Church and schisms of Syrian Orthodoxy.

In the '60s the church acquired a new direction from the

Psychedelic Movement, and for a while maintained a presence at T. Leary's commune in Millbrook, New York. At the same time the discovery of Sufism led certain of its members to undertake journeys to the East.

One of these Americans, known by the Moorish name Wali Fard, travelled for years in India, Persia, and Afghanistan, where he collected an impressive assortment of exotic initiations: Tantra in Calcutta, from an old member of the Bengali Terrorist Party; Sufism from the Ovayssi Order in Shiraz, which rejects all human masters and insists on visionary experience; and finally, in the remote Badakhshan Province of Afghanistan, he converted to an archaic form of Ismailism (the so-called Assassins) blended out of Buddhist Yab-Yum teachings, indigenous shamanic sorcery and extremist Shiite revolutionary philosophy-worshippers of the *Umm-al-kitab*, the "Matrix Book."

Up until the Soviet invasion of Afghanistan and the reactionary orthodox "revolution" in Iran, Fard carried on trade in carpets and other well-known Afghan exports. When history forced him to return to America in 1978, he was able to launder his savings by purchasing about 200 acres of land in the New Jersey Pine Barrens. Around the turn of the decade he moved into an old rod & gun club on the property along with several runaways from Paramus, New Jersey, and an anarchist lesbian couple from Brooklyn, and founded the Moorish Science Ashram.

Through the early-to-mid-'80s the commune's fortunes fluctuated (sometimes nearly flickering out). Fard self-published a series of Xeroxed "Visionary Recitals" in which he attempted a synthesis of heretical and antinomian spirituality, post-Situationist politics, and chaos science. After the Crash, a number of destitute Moors and sympathizers began turning up at the Ashram seeking refuge. Among them were two young chaos scientists recently fired from Princeton (on a charge of "seditious nonsense"), a brother and sister, Frank and Althea Dobbs.

The Dobbs twins spent their early childhood on a UFO-cult commune in rural Texas, founded by their father, a retired insurance salesman who was murdered by rogue disciples during a revival in California. One might say that the siblings had a head start in chaos — and the Ashram's modus vivendi suited them admirably. (The Pine Barrens have often been called "a perfect place for a UFO landing.") They settled into an old Airstream trailer and constructed a crude laboratory in a rebuilt barn hidden deep in the Pines. Illegal sources of income were available from agricultural projects, and the amorphous community took shape around the startling breakthroughs made by the Dobbs twins during the years around the end of the decade.

As undergraduates at the University of Texas the siblings had produced a series of equations which, they felt certain, contained the seeds of a new science they called "cognitive chaos." Their dismissal from Princeton followed their attempt to submit these theorems, along with a theoretical/philosophical system built upon them, as a joint PhD thesis.

On the assumption that brain activity can be modeled as a "fractal universe," an outré topology interfacing with both random and determined forces, the twins' theorems showed that consciousness itself could be presented as a set of "strange attractors" (or "patterns of chaos") around which specific neuronal activity would organize itself. By a bizarre synthesis of mandelbrot and Cantor, they "solved the problem" of n-dimensional attractors, many of which they were able to generate on Princeton's powerful computers before their hasty departure. While realizing the ultimately indeterminate nature of these "mind maps," they felt that by attaining a thorough (non-intuitive and intuitive) grasp of the actual *shapes* of the attractors, one could "ride with chaos" somewhat as a "lucid dreamer" learns to contain and direct the process of REM sleep. Their aborted thesis suggested a boggling array of benefits which might accrue from such links between cybernetic processes and awareness itself, including the exploration of the brain's unused capacities, awareness of the morphogentic field and thus conscious control of autonomic functions, mind-directed repair of tissue at the cellular/genetic level (control over most diseases and the aging process), and even a direct perception of the Heisenbergian behavior of matter (a process they called "surfing the wave function"). Their thesis advisor told them that even the most modest of these proposals would suffice for their expungement from the Graduate Faculty — and if the whole concept (including theorems) were not such obvious lunacy, he would have reported them to the FBI as well.

Two more scientists — already residents of Ong's Hat — joined with Fard and the twins in founding the Institute of Chaos studies. By sheer "chance" their work provided the perfect counterparts to the Dobbs' research. Harold Acton, an expatriate British computer — (and reality—) hacker, had already linked 64 second-hand personal computers into a vast ad-hoc system based on his own *I Ching* oriented speculations. And Martine Kallikak, a native of the Barrens from nearby Chatsworth, had set up a machine shop.

Ironically, Martine's ancestors once provided guinea pigs for a notorious study in eugenics carried out in the 1920s at the Vineland NJ State Home for the Insane. Published as a study in "heredity and feeblemindness," the work proclaimed poverty, non-ordinary sexuality, reluctance to hold a steady job, and enjoyment of intoxicants as *proofs* of genetic decay — and thus made a lasting contribution to the legend of bizarre and lovecraftian Piney backwoods people, incestuous hermits of the bogs. Martine had long since proven herself a *bricoleuse*, electronics buff and back-lot inventor of great genius and artistry. With the arrival of the Dobbs twins, she discovered her tre metier' in the realization of various devices for the implementation of their proposed experiments.

The synergy level at the ICS exceeded all expectations. Contacts with other underground experts in various related fields were maintained by "black modem" as well as personal visits to the Ashram. The spiritual rhythms permeating the place proved ideal: periods of dazed lazy contemplation and applied hedonics alternating with "peak" bursts of self-overcoming activity and focused attention. The hodgepodge of "Moorish Science" (Tantra, sufism, Ismaili esotericism, alchemy and psychopharmacology, bio-feedback and "brain machine" meditation techniques,etc.) seemed to harmonize in unexpectedly fruitful ways with the "pure" science of the ICS.

Under these conditions progress proved amazingly swift,

stunning even the Institutes founders. Within a year major advances had been made in all the fields predicted by the equations. Somewhat more than three years after founding there occurred *the* breakthrough, the discovery which served to re-orient our entire project in a new direction: the Gate.

But to explain the Gate we must retrace some step, and reveal exactly the purposes and goals of the ICS and Moorish Science Ashram — the curriculum upon which our activities are based, and which constitutes our *raison d'etre*.

The Curriculum

The original and still ultimate concern of our community is the enhancement of consciousness and consequent enlargement of mental, emotional and psychic activities. When the Ashram was founded by W.Fard the only means available for this work were the bagful of oriental and occultist meditational techniques he had learned in Central Asia, the first-generation "mind machines" developed during the '80s, and the resources of exotic pharmacology.

With the first successes of the Dobbs twin's research, it became obvious to us that the spiritual knowledge of the Ashramites could be re-organized into a sort of preparatory course of training for workers in "Cognitive Chaos." This does not mean we surrendered our original purpose — attainment of non-ordinary consciousness — but simply that ICS work could be viewed as a prolongation and practical application of the Ashram work. The theorems allow us to re-define "self liberation" to include physical self-renewal and life-extension as well as the exploration of material reality which (we maintain) remains *one* with the reality of consciousness. In this project, the kind of awareness fostered by meditational techniques plays a part just as vital as the *techne'* of machines and the pure mentation of mathematics.

In this scenario, the theorems — or at least a philosophical understanding of them — serve the purpose of an abstract *icon* for contemplation. Thus the theorems can be absorbed or englobed to the point where they become part of the inner structure (or "deep grammar") of the mind itself.

In the first stage, intellectual comprehension of the theorems parallels spiritual work aimed at refining the faculty of *attention*. At the same time a kind of psychic anchor is constructed, a firm grounding in celebratory body-awareness. The erotic and sensual for us cannot be ritualized and aimed at anything "higher" than themselves — rather, they constitute the very *ground* on which our dance is performed, and the atmosphere or *taste* which permeates our whole endeavor.

We symbolize this first course of work by the tripartite Sanskrit term *satchitananda*, "Being/consciousness/bliss" — the ontological level symbolized by the theorems, the psychological level by the meditation, the level of joy by our "tantrik" activity.

The second course (which can begin at any time during or after the first) involves practical instruction in a variety of "hard sciences", especially evolutionary biology and genetics, brain physiology, Quantum Mechanics and computer hacking. We have no need for these disciplines in any academic sense — in fact our work has already overturned many existing paradigms in these fields and rendered the textbooks useless for our purposes — so we have tailored these courses specifically for relevance to our central concern, and jettisoned everything extraneous.

At this point a Fellow of the ICS is prepared for work with the device we call the "egg." This consists of a modified sensory-deprivation chamber in which attention can be focused on a computer terminal and screen. Electrodes are taped to various body parts to provide physiological data which is fed into the computer. The explorer now dons a peculiar helmet, a highly sophisticated fourth-generation version of the early "brain machines," which can sonically stimulate brain cells either globally or locally and in various combinations, thus directing not only "brain waves" but also highly specific mental-physical functions. The helmet is also plugged into the computer and provides feedback in various programmed ways.

The explorer now undertakes a series of exercises in which the theorems are used to generate graphic animations of the "strange attractors" which map various states of consciousness, setting up feedback loops between this "iconography" and the actual states themselves, which are in turn generated through the helmet simultaneously with their representation on the screen. Certain of these exercises involve the "alchemical" use of mind-active drugs, including new vasopressin derivatives, beta-endorphins and hallucinogens (usually in "threshold" dosages). Some of these tinctures are simply to provide active-relaxation and focused-attention states, others are specifically linked to the requirements of "Cognitive Chaos" research.

Even in the earliest and crudest stages of the egg's development the ICS founders quickly realized that many of the Dobbs twins' PhD thesis predictions might be considered cautious or conservative. Enhanced control of autonomous body functions was attained even in the second-generation version, and the third provided a kind of bathysphere capable of "diving" down even to the cellular level. Certain unexpected side-effects included phenomena usually classified as paranormal. We knew we were not hallucinating all this, quite bluntly, because we obtained concrete and measurable results, not only in terms of "yogic powers" (such as suspended animation, "inner hear," lucid dreaming and the like) but also in observable benefits to health: rapid healing, remission of chronic conditions, absence of disease.

At this point in development of the egg (third generation) the researchers attempted to "descend" (like Sci-Fi micronauts) to the Quantum level.

Perhaps the thorniest of all Quantum paradoxes involves the "collapse of the wave function" — the state of Schroedinger's famous cat. When does a wave "become" a particle? At the moment of observation? If so, does this implicate human consciousness in the actual Q-structure of reality itself? By observing do we in effect "create?" The ICS team's ultimate dream was to "ride the wave" and actually experience (rather than merely observe) the function-collapse. Through "participation" in Q-events, it was hoped that the observer/observed duality could be overcome or evaded.

This hope was based on rather "orthodox" Copenhagian interpretations of Quantum reality. After some months of in-tensive work, however, no one had experienced the sought-for and expected "moment"...each wave seemed to flow as far as one cared to ride it, like some perfect surfer's curl extending to infinity. We began to suspect that the answer to the question "when?" might be "never!"

This contingency had been described rigorously in only one interpretation of Q-reality, that of J.Wheeler — who proved that the wave function need never collapse provided that every Q-event gives rise to an "alternating world" (the Cat is *both* alive and dead).

To settle this question a fourth generation of the egg was evolved and tested, while simultaneously a burst of research was carried out in the abstruse areas of "Hillbert space" and the topology of n-dimensional geometry, on the intuitive assumptions that new "attractors" could thereby be generated and used to visualize or "grok" the transitions between alternate universes.

Again the ICS triumphed...although the immediate success of the fourth-generation egg provoked a moment of fear and panic unmatched in the whole history of "Cognitive Chaos."

The first run-through of the "Cat" program was undertaken by a young staff-member of great brilliance (one of the original Paramus runaways) whose nickname happened to be Kit — and it happened to take place on the Spring Equinox. At the precise moment the heavens changed gears, so to speak, the entire egg vanished from the laboratory.

Consternation would be a mild term for what ensued. For about seven minutes the entire ICS lost its collective cool. At that point however the egg reappeared with its passenger intact and beaming...like Alice's Cheshire Cat rather than Schroedinger's poor victim.

He had succeeded in riding the wave to its "destination" — an alternate universe. He had observed it and — in his words — "memorized its address." Instinctively he felt that certain dimensional universes must act as "strange attractors" in their own right, and are thus far easier to access (more "probable") than others. In practical terms, he had not been dissolved but had found the way to a "universe next door."

The Gateway had been opened.

Where is Ong's Hat?

According to Piney legend, the village of Ong's Hat was founded sometime in the 19th century when a man named Ong threw his hat up in the air, landed it in a tree and was unable to retrieve it (we like to think it vanished into another world). By the 1920s all traces of settlement other than a few crumbling chimneys had faded away. But the name appealed so much to cartographers that some of them retained it — a dot representing nothing in the midst of the most isolated flat dark scrub-pines and sandy creeks in all the vast, empty and perhaps haunted Barrens.

W. Fard's acreage lies in the invisible suburbs of this invisible town, of which we are the sole inhabitants. You can find it easily on old survey maps, even trace out the the old dirt road leading into the bogs where a little square represents the decrepit "Ong's Hat Rod & Gun Club," original residence. However, you might discover that finding the ICS itself is not so simple.

If you compare your old survey map with the very latest, you will note that our area lies perilously close to the region infamous in recent years, the South Jersey Nuclear Waste Dump near Fort Dix. The "accident" that occurred there has made the Barrens even more empty and unpopular, as any hard-core Pineys fled the pollution melting into the state's last untouched wilderness. The electrified fence shutting off the deadly zone runs less than a mile above our enclave.

The Accident occurred while we were in the first stages of developing the fourth-generation egg, the Gate. At the time we had no idea of its full potential. However all of us, except for the very youngest (who were evacuated), had by then been trained in elementary self-directed generation. A few tests proved that with care and effort we could resist at least the initial onslaught of radiation sickness. We decided to stick it out, at least until "the authorities" (rather than the dump) proved too hot to endure.

Once the Gate was discovered, we realized the situation had been saved. The opening and actual interdimensional travel, can only be effected by a fully trained "cognitive chaote;" so the first priority was to complete the course for all our members. A technique for "carrying" young children was developed (it seems not to work for adult "non-initiates"), and it was discovered that all inanimate matter within the egg is also carried across with the operator.

Little by little we carted our entire establishment (including most of the buildings) across the topological abyss. Unlike Baudelaire who pleaded, "Anywhere! — so long as out of this world!" we knew where we were going. Ong's Hat has indeed vanished from New Jersey, except for the hidden laboratory deep in the backwoods where the gate "exists."

On the other side of the Gate we found a Pine Barrens similar to ours but in a world which apparently never developed human life. Of course we have since visited a number of other worlds, but we decided to colonize this one, our first Newfoundland. We still live in the same scattering of weather-gray shacks, Airstream trailers, recycled chicken coops, and mail-order yurts, only a bit more spread out — and considerably more relaxed. We're still dependent on your world for many things — from coffee to books to computers — and in fact we have no inclination of cutting ourselves off like anchorites and merely scampering into a dreamworld. We intend to spread the word.

The colonization of new worlds — even an infinity of them — can never act as a panacea for the ills of Consensus Reality — only as a palliative. We have always taken our diseases with us to each new frontier...everywhere we go we exterminate aborigines and battle with our weapons of law and order against the chaos of reality.

But this time, we believe, the affair will go differently — because this time the journey outward can only be made simultaneously with the journey inward-and because this bootstrap-trick can only be attained by a consciousness which, to a significant degree, has overcome itself, liberated itself from self-sickness-and "realized itself."

Not that we think ourselves saints, or try to behave morally, or imagine ourselves a super-race, absolved from good and evil. Simply, we like to consider ourselves awake when we're awake, sleeping when we sleep. We enjoy good health. We have learned that desire demands the *other* just as it demands the self. We see no end to growth while life lasts, no cessation of unfolding, of continual outpouring of form from chaos. We're moving on, nomads or monads of the dimensions. Sometimes we feel almost satisfied...at other times, terrified.

Meanwhile our agents of chaos remain behind to set up ICS courses, distribute Moorish Orthodox literature (a major mask for our propaganda) to subvert and evade our enemies...We haven't spoken yet of our enemies. Indeed there remains much we have not said. This text, *disguised as a sort of New Age vacation brochure*, must fall silent at this point, satisfied that it has embedded within itself enough clues for its intended readers (who are already halfway to Ong's hat in any case) but not enough for those with little faith to follow.

CHAOS NEVER DIED!

INCUNABULA 2.5

Advances in Skin Science: Quantum Tantra
An Interview with Nick Herbert
by Joseph Matheny

"It's always gooiest before it solidifies"
Beverly's Ovation
Beverly Rubik Ph.d

"Quantum Tantra is not just another way to get high using
common objects you can find around the
house...Caution: Practising Q.T. before you understand
Bell's Theorem of interconnectveness is like walking into
the Amazon jungle without a map."
Alternate Dimensions
Jabir ibn Hayyan

Journal entries
October 13, 1992

I finally get a line on INCUNABULA. Following a lead from a
culture-jamming club in San Francisco, I arrive in the small New Jersey
town of Ong's Hat. The address that I have for INCUNABULA is a
P.O. Box. The local postmaster/general store operator was very helpful.
Almost too helpful! He told me that Cranston and INCUNABULA
books had fled the area one night about a month ago. I gained access
to Cranston's P.O. box key while the owner had his back turned and
returned later to examine the contents. All I found inside were overdraft
notices from his bank and some solicitations from a church of geniuses
in Dallas, Texas or some such nonsense. Another dead end.

October 14, 1992

I arrive in New York City, get a room, restock supplies and think.
I call New Jersey information to get the phone number for the Ong's
Hat general store and post office so I can ask the postmaster a few
more questions. I am told by the inbred boob on the other end of the
line that there is no such town listed in New Jersey, and after a long

and heated debate, we terminate the phone call by mutually insulting each other's gene pool.

God, I hate the phone company.

October 16, 1992

Two days (and two bottles of Johnny Walker Black Label) later, I finally get a lead on one of the most intriguing authors listed in the INCUNABULA catalogue, Nick Herbert, author of *Quantum Reality, Faster Than Light: Superluminal Loopholes in Physics*, and of course, the legendary *Alternate Dimensions* . Herbert was a former SDI scientist turned renegade researcher. His past areas of renegade research involved pleasure dome technologies, Quantum Tantra (the Egg Yoke method), Time and Dimensional travel theories, and gelatinous substances.

I'll give you a little background on *Alternate Dimensions (A.D.)*. It was written in 1989 by Herbert, but was suppressed by the publisher, Harper & Row, for unexplained reasons in 1990 (see INCUNABULA & INCUNABULA 3).

INCUNABULA was offering bound, uncorrected galley copies for $100.00 each, or at least they were, until Cranston disappeared with the whole kit-n-kaboodle. In *A.D.*, it seems that Herbert gave away the inner secrets of a Tantric-dimensional travel cult based in northern California. Using techniques that combined Herbert's own theory of Quantum Tantra, and hardware technology, consisting of an egg-shaped craft of some sort, members of the cult were able to penetrate into other dimensions. There were also intense visualization techniques, and Tantric-Egg-Yoke postures involved, but the Xerox copy I had purchased from MediaKaos seemed to be missing some of the key technical portions.

Herbert was now hiding out in the backwater town of Boulder Creek, CA, deep in the heart of the Santa Cruz mountains. I hopped aboard a plane to San Jose, and drove a rental car up to Boulder Creek. About a mile away from Herbert's farm house, I called him on my cellular phone. Surprisingly enough, Herbert was very cordial, and agreed to meet me in town for lunch and conversation. He suggested Adelita's Mexican Cantina, gave me directions, and promised to meet me there in an hour. I drove into town and went over my notes while I waited.

About an hour later, Dr.Herbert appeared in the parking lot driving a electric Stutz Bearcat kit car. I recognized him instantly from his jacket photos, even with the recently acquired beard. Was he attempting to change his appearance? Was he preparing to flee, like Cranston had 30 days ago? I casually reached into my jacket and activated my pocket recorder. I waved him over to my table, and after shaking hands we settled down to a lunch of Dos Equis and Gorditas.

"Okay," I said, after some pleasantries about the weather, "let's start with the obvious question: What is Quantum Tantra?"

"Well, psychology has used a lot of classic metaphors to explain the mind, like the hydraulic metaphor of urges building up, and even when repressed, they'll find some way to spurt out to the surface. We're told that releasing your repressions will relieve the pressure, and you'll become healthy. That's a very classical metaphor. Now we have this marvelous new way of thinking called quantum mechanics, and it seems right to use these metaphors to explain human behavior. So, what's the most interesting human behavior of all? Sexual, of course. That's the idea, to use quantum mechanical metaphors to explore sexuality, to look at it through the lens of quantum physics. I would consider Q.T. successful if we could find new things to do that never would have been thought, of using the old metaphors. I mean, of course, pleasant things (laughter). The core idea of Q.T. stems from Heisenberg's statement that "atoms are not things." So, Q.T. naturally extrapolated that statement into "well then people are not things, either." People are not things in the same way that atoms are not things."

"What are things?" I asked

"Things are entities that have attributes, whether you look at them or not. They're big, they're solid and such. You can list their attributes. Non-things, or Quantum objects, like atoms or molecules, don't have attributes. They are basically clusters of oscillating possibilities, the possibilities not even being well-defined. It might reward us to look that way at people, as oscillating possibilities."

He took a long draw off his Dos Equis, and signaled the waiter for another.

"So, try and think of what the essence of quantum theory is," he continued. "Three adjectives: randomness, thinglessness, and interconectiveness. Randomness I associate with the spontaneity that is within people. Uncertainty is the very essence of romance. It's what you don't know that intrigues you."

"Now, thinglessness is even more renunciatory," he went on. "The notion of treating people like possibilities rather than fixed structures is a healthy one, I think."

"Interconnectiveness is the most fantastic feature of Q.T. Things are connected in the quantum world in such a way that only did we not think of it before the discovery of quantum mechanics, but I don't think we could have thought this way at all. It's so strange. The terrestrial belief system that comes the closest to quantum connectiveness is Voodoo."

"Sympathetic magick?" I queried. This was getting good.

"Yes, sympathetic magick," he replied.

"Of course, the Voodoo conception is naive in comparison to Q.T.'s connectiveness. In Voodoo, you do something like burn someone's hair to give them a headache. The Quantum connection isn't that crude. It has more to do with timing. In the Quantum world, you burn someone's hair, and maybe they miss an appointment. The Newtonian world view emphasized control over the world, whereas, the Quantum world view doesn't emphasize control so much as timing. You could say that the Newtonian view emphasized force, where the Quantum world emphasizes finesse."

"One analogy is ordinary steerable dish radar versus phased array antennae. Steerable dish physically moves the whole antenna structure. In the phased array antennae, you have a whole array that are all fixed. None of them move, but by changing the timing on these antennae, you get a virtual antenna that's pointed in any direction. That's an example of finesse, rather than force. Quantum connection is like that. It is set up like Voodoo by having something that the other person has interacted with, some sympathetic object."

"But what does this have to do with sex?" I asked.

Herbert was quick to answer. "I'm getting to that. In Q.T., the Tantra part has to do with sex as well as religion. Every religion has their symbol. The Christians have the cross, Islam has the crescent and star, the Pagans have the pentagram, the wheel for Buddhism, and so forth. Q.T. has it's symbols, also. One of them is this fork."

He picked up a salsa-encrusted fork, and stared at it rapturously.

"It reminds us to see the world as possibilities," he continued. "In the Newtonian world, starting from now, only one thing could happen. Q.T. sees the future as open possibilities, like the tines of this fork. Actually, if this fork were fuzzy, like Man Ray's fuzzy cup and spoon..."

I was beginning to understand. That or the Dos Equis was kicking in. I felt lightheaded.

"So the borders would not quite be defined..." I replied.

"Yes," he said, eyes twinkling in the candlelight. "The possibilities are defined only by your intentions, by how you construe the moment. Quantum possibilities are not quite as defined as dice possibilities even. With a die, only one of six numbers will come up, whereas with Quantum possibilities, it depends on how you look at the moment, and that again, is part of thinglessness. All of these elements have resonances in popular literature. Like the talk of the inexplicable chemistry that occurs between two people, or this notion of 'it's bigger than both of us'. The type of connectivity that's possible in quantum theory allows two connected entities to be in indefinite states , but allows the couple itself to be in a definite state! The mathematics on this are clear. As Heisenberg said, 'quantum theory has changed our way of thinking completely,' and it's changed in such a way that it didn't dissolve into some unclear fuzzy fog but into this absolute clarity of a new mathematics. Now, the mathematics describe the fog in a very precise way. So, it's this kind of very precise unclarity."

"You're talking like a lot of mystics I know!" I scoffed.

He replied laughing, "Except, this is found in ordinary physics! This is stuff that was discovered 75 years ago. It's not new stuff at all. It's only now beginning to permeate popular culture. So, we have this system where each member of the pair, say, a man and a woman, or a man and a man, or a woman and a woman, or whatever, are defined. They've gotten themselves into a state where their individualities are not as clear, but the couple itself as an entity, is better defined

113

than the individual members of the set. We use symbols, like the fork, to remind ourselves of these things, because the human mind is not yet used to thinking in parallels."

"Our data rate is miniscule compared to say, television data rates equivalent to megabits per second, or telephones, which are equivalent to thousands of kilobits per second. Morse code is about 10 bits per second, and that's pretty close to our attention rate! I mean, when we're not on robot, when we do come to attention, we don't bring much to this moment in terms of quantity. It's been estimated at about 16 bits a second. So, people need simple graphic symbols, like the fork, or the cross, or the crescent, to remind themselves that they're Moslems, or whatever. So, one symbol I've invented to epitomize Randomness, Thinglessness and Interconnectiveness is the trinity of White, Hot and Sticky. White corresponds to Thinglessness, Hot to Randomness, and Sticky to Interconnectiveness. By white, I mean like white light, all the colors together, all human sexual potentials. Thinglessness is wrought with possibilities. As David Finklestein, the inventor of quantum logic said, 'We are all white light, in the sense that we are all possibilities.' Hot has to do with newness, spontaneity that we can bring to the moment to remind us that the moment can be ever new. That's a hard thing to live up to sexually, and otherwise. Sticky, of course, typifies the new kind connectiveness. A metaphor for achieving stickyness are objects that you break in two and each partner keeps one half. The fracture is unique, that I will only match one other person in the whole world! Quantum objects help to enhance this two-person white, hot, sticky state. And music is the connection in this technology."

"Why music?" I asked.

"Because, these possibilities are vibratory," he answered. "In the physical world, every atom, or possibility is vibrating at a certain frequency. The higher the energy level, the higher the frequency or pitch of the vibrations. We can't hear, smell, see, or taste any of these vibrations except indirectly. I'm doing more research with solid state technology, sound sequences."

"Ok, now what about *Alternate Dimensions*, the egg craft, the travel cults, Tantric-Yoke techniques, I mean, what about all this stuff!" I finally blurted, unable to hold back any longer.

"Young man, I have no idea what you're talking about. All I can say is there are some questions that you should not ask directly, and some answers that may come as a result of finesse over force".

"This interview is now concluded."

Incunabula 3.0

Joseph Matheny Interviews the Elusive Emory Cranston

Journal entry

1/23/94

After interviewing Nick Herbert and being stuck with the check for lunch, I discovered that Mr. Herbert had scribbled a phone number on the back of the receipt before leaving. It was a New Jersey exchange. I recognized it almost instantly, and underneath it, the letters E.C. were scrawled. Finally, a lead ! This had to be the phone number for none other than Emory Cranston, proprietor of INCUNABULA books. So, Cranston was still on Earth Prime, and accessible by phone. I went back to my motel room and dialed the number.

[ring]

[ring]

EC: Hello?

JM: Hi, is this Emory Cranston ?

EC: Who wants to know ?

JM: My name is Joseph Matheny. I got your phone number from Nick Herbert. I'm a reporter investigating the Ong's Hat story, and I thought you might give me some insight into where you came across all the material in INCUNABULA. I got the catalogue from a group of Culture Hackers in San Francisco.

(silence)

Is this Emory Cranston ?

EC: Who did you say you were again ?

JM: A freelance investigative reporter doing a story on the travel cults and the Ong's Hat Institute.

EC: And who gave you this phone number ?

JM: Nick Herbert. I was trying to find out where INCUNABULA is located now.

EC: (Audible sigh on other end of line) Oh, well. At least he could have warned me. But it doesn't really matter...after all, there's no "here" here anyway, so I won't be here tomorrow. Does that answer your first question ?

JM: You mean INCUNABULA is located in "virtual space"?

EC: As far as your concerned, yes.

JM: Well, in the introduction to the INCUNABULA catalogue, you stated that you had uncovered "...a conspiracy so deep that no other researcher has yet become aware of it (outside of certain intelligence circles, needless to say)..." Is that still true? Why hasn't this become a more popular conspiracy theory? How did you come across this information?

EC: No, it's no longer true. Since I published the catalogue, everything has changed. Everything ! And look, this is no longer a "theory." I admit, when I first published, I really didn't know jack-shit about anything. Yes, I was a "conspiracy theorist", how pathetic ! Let me ask you, what kind of epistemological black hole...I mean, if the conspiratoligists "know" anything it wouldn't be a "theory" anymore, would it? It'd be "fact." Who killed Kennedy? Where are the UFOs from? They don't "know", do they?

JM: You have answers to these questions ?

EC: Pal, I've got lots of answers! Alternative answers. Get it? But that's not important. You ask why "my theory" isn't better known or more "popular" ? Why aren't they discussing it at UFO conferences, eh? Why isn't it on TV? Well, there's an easy answer to that. The truth is never popular, and it's never seen on TV! You know in your heart I'm right about this don't you? If you think about what's really important to you, you'll realize it's not popular and it's never been seen on TV (or if it has...well then I'm sorry for you). It's true, when I first came across the information...I was living in Chatsworth, in the Pine Barrens, near Ong's Hat...I was doing a catalogue...Tesla, Reich, Bioshamanics, Hollow Earth, crop circles, Mae Brussell...that sort of thing. Strange stories were circulating about the Institute out at Ong's Hat. They wouldn't talk to me. Then they disappeared. That's when I got "really" interested and began collecting the literature. A few years later, I published the catalogue to see if they'd get in touch with me. I wanted to flush them out. I wanted to know.

JM: So what happened?

EC: Let's just say I succeeded in stirring the shit beyond my wildest expectations. You know, most conspiratologists would die of shock if they suddenly received proof that their theories were real. You'll notice that not one UFO "expert" has ever been abducted. And not one Kennedy-Conspiracy nut has ever been assassinated. These things happen to other people, not to Conspiracy Theorists, right? Well, let's just say...that's what I mean when I say...this isn't a "theory" anymore.

JM: Do you feel endangered in anyway, being so outspoken about info that has obviously gotten some people killed? How do you deal with the danger? What precautions have you taken? Why are you talking to me for example?

EC: Why am I talking to you? There are reasons...reasons you don't really need to know. Just go ahead and do what ever you intend to do. Publish. But be careful. At this point, the cat's out of the bag, as Alice Schroedinger's would say (laughs). I doubt they...I don't think anyone would bother anymore...it's gone so far beyond that. Now, as to my state of savvy when I published the INCUNABULA catalogue...you know how conspiracy buffs like to pretend they're running a great risk...that hidden forces will try to silence them, blah blah. So buy my stuff now, before it's too late, etc., etc. Not one of them really believes it. I didn't believe it. I was extremely fortunate. The catalogue fell into the right hands...just about five minutes before it fell into the wrong hands. I was contacted. I was protected. Literally whisked away. In the nick of time. Next question, please.

JM: But...

EC: No no no. Read the catalogue. Think about it. Chances are you'll figure it out. You were smart enough to find this phone number, after all. That's why I'm talking to you. Next question.

JM: Ok. How many books have you sold? How many people do you think you've convinced?

EC: I'm not really running the catalogue anymore. It can't be suppressed-it's out there, it's circulating. But I'm not selling the books now. Those who need the books, get the books. I don't need the money, after all. Those who can really read the catalogue and figure out the next step...well, not everything in INCUNABULA is accurate, of course. But the clues are there. Follow the garden of forking paths. Ah, how many, you ask? I can tell you exactly. The answer is precisely 16 people have followed the thread so far. We're aware of another dozen or so who are working on it. At a certain point in their researches they'll be helped...if possible. One may blunder, you see. Some tracks lead to the Minotaur, know what I mean? And some of those dozen or so are working for the wrong people. They won't be helped.

JM: How did you obtain the more "esoteric" material, like *Alternate Dimensions* by "Jabir ibn Hayaan" aka Nick Herbert?

EC: Oh, *Alternate Dimensions* can hardly be called one of the more "esoteric" titles in the list. After all, Herbert was still a Theorist when he wrote it. The book is actually wrong on a number of points, though quite brilliant as an approach. The fact is, I tracked down Dr. Herbert when I was assembling the catalogue. I'd read his other work and realized he must be heading in the right direction. At first he wouldn't talk to me at all. He suspected I was an agent of whatever Shadowy Forces were trying to suppress the book and succeeding. From various angry remarks he dropped I was able to piece together the story. His manuscript and files had been stolen right out of his house, and the publishers refused to return their copies or any of the page proofs. They were stonewalling him. So I...well, I stole it.

JM: What?

EC: I went to the publisher. I had a very strong intuition as to which group was blocking publication. I posed as an agent of that group. Apparently I was correct, and it seems I knew enough to convince the publisher of my *bona fide*s so to speak. He was so glad to hand over the book you'd've thought it was a bomb! Later he was fired. I suppose he's lucky to be alive, the schmuck. I copied the proofs and returned the originals to Dr. Herbert. He agreed to let me list it. After all, it was the only way his work was ever going to be distributed. Of course it's a moot point now. I mean, the book is seriously out-of-date and there's not going to be a revised edition.

JM: Well, it's obvious that you've been in contact with some of the travel cult members. Can you tell me who?

EC: That would be telling.

JM: Aw, come on! This is not turning out to be much of an interview.

EC: Nonsense, young man. What I'm giving you is gold, pure gold. All right, then...would it surprise you to hear that you've already met a fair number of "cult members"? The heiress in the Berkeley Hills who knows all about Tarantula venom? That Irish humorist who lives in James Joyce's Martello tower in Howth, outside Dublin? The aging psychedelic guru...the so called Persian Anarchist...the so called Satanic rock-star...the Montana cowboy-secret-agent-hacker...the cyberpunk Sci-Fi Surrealist...

JM: No ! They would've told me...

EC: Guess again.

JM: I believe you're...you're disinforming me here, Mr. Cranston.

EC: Check it out.

JM: I will.

EC: Do. Next question.

JM: Um, ok. Uh...what new information have you come across since the catalogue was published? What new developments have there been in this "science" of travel?

EC: I can't really tell you that. "Cult member" means nothing now. All the players know who the other players are. I'm not giving anything away. But...new developments on the tech end? No. Certain people could gain an edge just from a vague description...well, I can tell you a few things. A paper came out right after my catalogue, so it's not listed, but everyone knows about it by now. It's by Suhrawardi. It's called *Not the Egg, the Joke*, a bad pun on yoga. Eggless travel has become S.O.P. for advanced Travellers. Some permanent doorways have been constructed which work even for non-initiates, sort of like *The Lion, the Witch, and the Wardrobe*. They're very nicely camouflaged. Fu Manchu couldn't do better. And, of course, they're guarded.

JM: Raiders of the Lost Ark...

EC: Eh? Oh yes...booby trapped. Definitely. It's a zero-sum game I'm afraid. Either you're on the bus or you're not on the bus. The Gateways...that's what we call them. The Gateways have to be there for those few who, shall we say, solve the catalogue without any help from any group. People that smart do exist — I have to admit I wasn't one of them! I compiled the catalogue and even I didn't "get it" ! But people who are capable of such...such quantum jujitsu, are people we need. For them the Gateways aren't guarded, but protected. As for the others who might somehow locate the transnational nexi...well, you know who I mean...

JM: No, who?

EC: The Tri-Lateral Commission! Read the catalogue! Figure it out! Who knows? Maybe you'll need to know one of these days.

JM: Is the secret government still active in this area, and if so what do they hope to achieve?

EC: Are you implying that because a "liberal" regime has taken over from a "conservative" regime that you people are free of "secret government"? Haven't you heard of the present leader's fascination with "virtual reality"? Where do you suppose power comes from, an "Invisible College" of "Illuminati"? (I use the terms metaphorically, of course.) Nothing has changed...only gotten hotter. In Baghdad...no, forget I said that. Scratch that. Dump the whole file. Next?

JM: Hmmmm, ok. Have you been to Earth2 or any of the other "worlds" and is this where you've been hiding?

EC: Well, no harm in telling you I suppose. Yes, in fact I've been spending quite a lot of time in Java2. It's not even a security thing anymore, really. Or not always. The truth is that, well, you can't possibly imagine a whole world for a utopia, complete with flora, fauna, picturesque ruins, and maybe, oh, ten people per square continent. Fresh air ! That alone is enough to...a universe next door, let's go ! (was it e.e.cummings who said that?)

JM: And if that one gets too crowded?

EC: Precisely. A number of Davy Crockett types have already "moved on" where they can't see the smoke of their neighbors fires, to put it mildly. We have no idea of the extent of the Series it may be "infinite" for all practical (or impractical) purposes.

JM: Why not just tell everybody, then?

EC: Would you want to be responsible for infecting the halls of infinity with, say the L.A. Police? Do you think the Pentagon deserves infinity? And what if it isn't infinite, etcetera?

JM: Who were the occupants of Java2 , that left behind the ruins?

EC: Well, that's the biggest news of all really. We found them — or rather they've found us. They claim to be an alternative evolutionary branch of Homo Sapiens through h.Javanesis and h.Neanderthalensis. They look like they're descended from lemurs rather than chimps, like us. A bit like the characters from Javanese shadow puppet plays. They discovered how to travel long ago, in a time we might think of as the time of Atlantis or Mu (only we would be wrong.) It's all rather Lovecraftian in as much as they claim to be responsible for certain aspects of human culture, aspects which are uncanny but not maleficent. Not only in Java — the Tuartha de Danaan of Ireland who vanished "underground", and other "faery" and "hollow earth" clues...the whole idea of another physical world, not a heaven or hell, but a Magickal universe next door...anyway, we were wrong about them travelling in time, either fast forward or backward. They simply set out to explore the Series. They think it may be endless, and some decided to return "home" to Java2. They're a completely non-hierarchic segmentary society, like primitive hunter/gatherers, but with a highly evolved culture. A lot of Terrans have completely "converted" to their way of life, even their language. You should hear their music! The returnees brought back some of their artifacts and...well, "furniture," I guess you'd call it. Their ancestors built a city during a "High Civilization" period in their history, but they rejected hard technology for cognitive sciences long ago. Our travel techniques are crude by comparison and lacking their whole mythopoetic value system. We're planning soon to release certain archival material here in Earth Prime, certain bits of art and music which we expect to act in a viral fashion to produce profound paradigm shifts. The traveller's culture is now, I believe, our most effective "weapon".

JM: So what's your bottom line — is this all co-creative or what?

EC: A smartass question.

JM: No, really.

EC: Who can say? What about our own cosmic locale, our own provincial reality? You can't make it go away by ceasing to believe in it. "Give me a place to stand and I'll move the world" but there is no noplace-place, no "outside" vantage point, from which to challenge consensus reality. "Magick" is notoriously difficult and vague, and terribly incremental — the utopian imagination seems futile. Reforms of consciousness appear to fail, unless they implement the emergence of new ruling classes or elites. "Religion" is a perfect case in point. But was religion the cause of "civilization" or the effect? Now...however, you see...it's a whole new game. There is an "outside" now, maybe an infinite number of outsides, places to stand with a lever in one hand and a magic mushroom in the other. The dispossessed have always believed in a millennium, a magickal resistance, a heaven on earth, a world turned upside down. This is it. Well, time's up.

JM: I had a million more questions. In fact...

EC: This phone number and address will become inoperative. Don't call us, we'll call you. And don't worry. The Reality check is in the mail.

[click]

(JM's note: the phone was indeed disconnected the next day, and the premises it was registered to vacated with no forwarding address left)

Survivors

As is so often the case with this type of research, you put the information out there and many come forward claiming to be *experiencers* of the phenomena you are describing. In 1999, Joseph Matheny returned from a 7 year self-imposed exile. Upon his return to public life, he was immediately besieged by many claiming to have been on the Ong's Hat Ashram or to have known such people. Peter Moon will cover much of this in his upcoming book on the Ong's Hat subject. What follows is a transcript of a phone interview with two individuals who went by the names of Rupert and Abel. These two individuals claim to have grown up in the Ong's Hat Ashram and describe an often repeated version of its demise. Also, a photojournal is included of a follow up meeting where Joseph was allowed to photograph an artifact said to have been used in dimensional travel training.

Rupert: ...every time I try to talk to him over the phone I get cut off. It's very suspicious. I wouldn't trust him for a second.

JM: Well, I did an interview with some aspiring yellow journalist back in August of last year and the same thing happened where, right when I was giving out some information, the phone circuits went dead and when I tried to call her back, actually, all I got was, "Circuit busy, circuit busy," for, like, an hour.

Rupert: For crying out loud, it's the year 2000. I mean, this kind of stuff shouldn't be going on, you know what I mean? I'm very suspicious about all this. This is something... Now, Abel and I don't discuss this that often, but this is a rare instance in which we've both agreed to talk again over the phone and, you know? I don't know. That's all I have to say.

JM: Abel, before you got cut off.... Are you there?

Abel: Yeah.

JM: Okay, he's there. Before you got cut off, I was actually doing a round robin of questions and I wanted to ask you, when you were on the Ong's Hat Ashram, and you guys were kids I know, but did you actually physically see one of the travel devices known as an Egg that was supposedly housed at the Ong's Hat Ashram?

Abel: I did. I didn't know... I knew it was...

Abel: ...supposed to fuck with or anything.

JM: Uh huh.

Abel: It was sort of, ah...

JM: It was off-limits to the kids?

Abel: Not off-limits per se. I mean, nobody would shoo us away per se, but it was very, uh, from what I...

Rupert: For crying out loud, Abel!

Abel: From what I knew then, this was very much sort of out in the open; it was, like, very low key. Everybody knew about it. Nobody really talked about it. Nobody really felt it was... they didn't really hide it. I don't remember there being much of a security issue around it.

JM: Right. So you were there during the military invasion, attack, intervention, whatever you want to call it?

Abel: Yeah, yeah. For most of it.

JM: Yeah, well now, what we've heard so far is that some nondescript helicopters appeared; some cables came out; some soldiers came down. They were carrying weapons and flamethrowers. They were basically there to eradicate something. Obviously, they've done a really good job of eradicating a lot of evidence that there was even an ashram there. I know that most of the buildings there were actually Airstream trailers and things like that, so that wouldn't be too hard to do, but I know that there were some structures there. I've actually been there and seen some of the foundations of some of the structures that are left behind. You know, you have to kind of go digging around for them, but...

Abel: Yeah.

JM: What do you think was the purpose of that, that attack?

Abel: Well, did you ask Mr. Bigsby yet?

JM: Yeah, I did. He went into it a little bit, just briefly described it. I can tell that he's a little perturbed right now that you're being a little more open about some things than he was, so....

Rupert: Well, I don't know about that. I mean, so now that the Egg's hatched, so to speak, I mean, I guess we might as well, you know, we might as well let everyone in – what is it, Danish? No, Denmark?

Abel: Mr. Bigsby is a little bit younger than me, if I remember.

Rupert: That's not true. I'm 33 years old. You understand, I'm

33 years old. I was the one that was the leader of the youth group back then. You understand.

Abel: Yeah, but I wasn't in the youth group, if you remember. I kind of...

Rupert: He keeps changing the story every time we do these kind of interviews.

Abel: I don't feel as protective talking about the Egg stuff because I don't feel that anyone's really.... It was really a side thing for me there. It wasn't really....

Rupert: Yeah, go on, Abel. Go on with your story. Yeah, that's fine.

Abel: ...more dogmatic people seem to have at this point.

JM: Well, okay, so you've got a different perspective. Maybe it seems like you were a little more detached from the purpose of the ashram. I mean, you were a kid.

Abel: Maybe I can get into it a little later, but like the attack I definitely remember. It was pretty bad, and I don't think it was just my perception of it being, you know, that I was still under ten at the time, seven, eight, nine, I don't exactly remember. But it was a pretty bad attack by anybody's standards I think, and the helicopters were the thing I remember because we heard them – I heard them, out playing – for a good ten minutes before they actually arrived. So that was something that stuck in my mind....

JM: So there's a lot of them?

Abel: Yeah. Yeah, there's a lot of them, and they were pretty... they weren't just, you know, your traffic helicopters, they were pretty high-grade military. They were heavy-duty, looked like they could move a lot of troops or a lot of equipment around.

Rupert: ...Just ain't true.

Abel: And the thing I remember about the soldiers – or troops; I don't know if you could call them soldiers; they weren't dressed quite like normal soldiers. But it felt like they – and again, perceptions of a kid change, you know over time. I don't know if I'm remembering this right. But even though they were, like, mostly, like, Caucasian, I didn't get the impression that they were American or that they even spoke English which was a strange thing.

JM: It's almost like it was a NATO force or a UN force.

Abel: It had that feel, like it was.... I always thought about that, and thought that it was foreign troops that came in, that maybe no American troops wanted to a sort of action like that, or maybe it was easier to cover up, or maybe, you know, it wasn't violating whatever Geneva Conventions there are, you know. It's all very strange.

Rupert: Let's just put it out right in the open right now. Let's just get it out in the open. The whole reason that thing happened in the first place was these people were tipped off. I mean, we all know that. Come on now.

Abel: Who's tipped off?

Rupert: These people — these soldiers — were tipped off. Where were they from? I don't know.

Abel: Yeah they were tipped off. I mean they don't just fly around looking for small....

Rupert: Yeah, but the fact of the matter is, I mean, they weren't tipped off by the US Government. They were tipped off by somebody else.

Abel: Yes, by the US Government. You'd have to be a moron not to come to that conclusion in the first second. But the point is, is that they weren't a US force, I don't think. It was like they brought in United Nations soldiers, like maybe they said, "Hey, Russia, we'll attack a village for you if you send these soldiers over here and attack some of our people." That's kind of what it seemed like to me. I don't know if that happened.

Rupert: These people just... they did not speak English well. Yes, that's true.

Abel: No, but they were mostly white, you know? They looked like, until you got close and saw the uniforms and saw the more European features and the non-English speaking, you knew something was strange.

Rupert: They were definitely not Danish, let me tell you right now. They were definitely not Danish.

JM: Did they have any kind of unusual insignia, or did they have any insignia on their uniforms?

Abel: I remember that most didn't but some, some did. They seemed to have something to do with stars, sort of a design, like red stars on black. But I don't really know what the stars meant. It wasn't a written language that I could, like, remember. Unless it was something that was symbols that I didn't know was a language.

JM: Right.

Rupert: From my understanding, it's just very similar to foot troops, secret foot troops from the old uniform of the Soviet Union army kind of uniform.

Abel: The uniform, you mean?

Rupert: Yeah, that's right.

Abel: They were. They definitely did seem Russian, which was weird, that not only were they foreign troops, but that they were wearing another, foreign uniform.

Rupert: It was definitely a mixed crowd in there, that's for sure, maybe. I mean it's definitely hard to say whether they were exactly Russian. There's different voices.

Abel: Yeah, yeah, that's true. I mean, it seemed like they attack in units that kept to themselves. Like it was very organized, very...

Rupert: Now as to their weapons, though, from my understanding most of them were semiautomatic.

Abel: Yeah, they were very high-grade military for the time. I mean, they weren't coming in with slingshots, that's for sure.

Rupert: They were definitely coming in with semi...I mean, the first thing we noticed were the semiautomatic weapons. I mean, when you show away to children semiautomatic weapons, you know, they're the first ones to fret. Men kind of tried to keep their cool, at least they appeared to. And my family, definitely the women and the children, were the first ones to see the soldiers, more or less, and....

Abel: You were mostly at a different end. You were at the north part.

Rupert: I don't know what you're talking about. I have no idea what he's... there's no north part/south part. I just remember that...

Abel: I have no conflict of what the actual directions were.

Rupert: I don't understand what you're talking about, but I do know this: that whatever it came down to, you know, was definitely on the record, and whatever we talk about it now, it's probably pretty much as I said it earlier, the Egg is hatched so to speak, the Egg is cracked. So in terms of what actually went down afterwards, it's speculation, and you know which is why the ashram disbanded, you know, the whole thing was a traumatic experience. Everyone went their own ways. Everyone left Jersey. A loose number kept in contact, and then at one point, everybody was talking to each other again. And then, close older members of the ashram passed on, and as a new generation of us just don't keep in touch and here we are.

JM: How did you get away? Or did they let you go?

Rupert: We were dismissed by two guards that were originally supposed to take in a convoy the women and children, and we were... all I remember as a child is that we were left at what was kind of like a housing facility for just women and children, split up from father, of course. And later on, of course, we were reunited with the rest of our families. You know, some of the older... my older brother, for example, was also separated from us, and we were regrouped. Things weren't quite the same though, let me tell you. I mean, growing up as a kid, you know, we never talked about the ashram. We would keep in touch with everyone, but we just wouldn't talk about the ashram, we wouldn't talk about what happened. The whole incident, it was all hush-hush, you know? We all moved on with our lives. Some of us still keep in touch. We're kind of restarting, like you know the kind of thing. I mean, our parents were hippies, you know, and the whole reason this ashram business started in the first place was because our parents were physicists all studying physics in college.

Abel: Mr. Bigsby, if that's your name, your parents were physicists there?

JM: You two.... Can I interject for a minute? *(telephone tones)*

Rupert: Hold on a second. Let me try and figure out what's going on there.

JM: You two seem like you're almost suspicious of each other.

Abel: I thought everybody knew most of this stuff, and he's the one who keeps saying the Egg is hatched, and I just, you know.... Maybe it's because I wasn't really included and my surviving family wasn't really included in a lot of these groups which he talks about, people getting together afterwards, you know, like survivors and whatever contacting each other. I think people still have an interest in it, I mean, we've had some contacts, but not much, and I don't know why we would.... Well, you know, I have an idea because of those other projects which were going on there, which had nothing to do with the Egg....

JM: What were those? What other projects?

Abel: Well, I mean, there were different ones, but I mean you...about the one that my parents were involved with.... Hang on one second. I gotta.... *(Abel speaks about a CB radio in the background)*

JM: He's actually talking to us from his shop!

Rupert: Well, you know, I mean, that's where Abel usually spends most of his time, so, you know....

Abel: Yeah, I mean, I'll explain the CB radio thing and the money thing later because you guys probably thought, and I know anybody listening to this or reading this probably thought, "Gee, this guy must be a real idiot, in this day and age, to be devoting his time to CBs what with the Internet, computer stuff happening." I'll get into that in a minute and show you I'm not an idiot like you were thinking.

JM: Okay.

Rupert: Well, you've got to understand, it's telecommunications industry's where it's at, man. I mean...

Abel: Otherwise we wouldn't be talking.

Rupert: It's the year 2000! Wake up! I mean, I don't understand it. He's up to something, let me tell you. We are suspicious of each other. I mean, everybody in the ashram, even though we still talk to each other, there's still a little bit of hesitancy, you know what I mean?

JM: Well, yeah, 'cause I guess that maybe you still think that one of the... the rat-out was maybe an inside job.

Rupert: Well, exactly, I mean, we're still trying to speculate.... Most of us here know who it is. I mean, I've got, you know, we've got some very close people, a few of us working together, and there's different ends of the whole thing. I mean, everybody has their own take on it.

Abel: I'm still not convinced it wasn't an accident. I mean, you know, with information leaking out, we, ah....

Rupert: Well, nobody knows who's talking to who anymore, I mean, you know? That's why I'm very conscious about these things.

Abel: My theory – and I could be wrong on this; I was young at the time and I really don't remember – is that with the project my parents were working on, which was the.... I'm not sure, because like I said, you were in a different part of the camp even if you don't seem to remember it, Mr. Bigsby, and we didn't really intermingle.

Rupert: Unbelievable.

Abel: What?

Rupert: Nothing. Nothing, nothing, nothing, nothing. You just keep going on. I'm sorry, I didn't mean to interrupt. Now apparently I'm refreshing your memory here a bit. But we really... my parents weren't physicists, unlike yours. We weren't really there for the Egg. Like I say, I was a kid, so I really had nothing to do with the Egg. But we... my parents, if you remember the tower, it wasn't very big, but I guess it was a short-wave radio big enough to do a good job. But my parents were running the numbers stations out of there. If you remember...

Rupert: Well, yeah, that's right, your parents were in the tower, that's right.

Abel: What?

Rupert: Nothing. I'm not going to repeat myself. Just keep going on.

Abel: I'd like you to repeat that. I don't know what you just said.

Rupert: Your parents were the oddballs of the lot. Everybody knows that.

Abel: They weren't physicists. We weren't involved in....

Rupert: That's right. Nobody.... Exactly right.

JM: Well, my understanding from Emory Cranston is that part of the scope of the project was to divide the ashram somewhat equally between physicists and artists. Is that...

Rupert: Well, yeah. Like I said, there were hippies, and there were physicists. I mean, you know, you can't have both. I mean they were. It's all during the six... I mean, it's all during that whole era. I mean, the sixties, seventies, you know, everybody walking around with big bellbottoms, and they all looked like hippies. But yeah, there's definitely some of them that were very well educated, and some of them that were, you know, into the whole experience of the ashram, more or less.

Abel: And they were stinky, if I remember. But I think, getting back to what I think happened, I know most survivors think that there was an informant. But I think that there was some sort of a weird, sort of quantum double-cross, if you will. The codes which were being transmitted — now I'm not sure if everybody here is familiar with the numbers stations, short-wave radio....

JM: Yeah, I am. Let me go ahead and describe it just a bit for the listeners. There are these strange radio stations that show up on different spectrums of the bandwidth in the short-wave spectrum and some other spectrums — UHF used to be one of them- and there a number of transmissions — a lot of them come out of the UK, some out of Russia, different places like that. And it's speculated, and actually even recently it's been admitted by a couple of organizations inside of different governments that those numbers being transmitted there are actually codes that are being sent to and from agents — spies, if you will — in different countries. And that's how they communicate.

Rupert: It's *Mother Night* all over again.

JM: Am I correct in that assessment?

Abel: That's more or less correct. The reason being is that short-wave radios are easy to carry and troops out in the field don't have much risk from listening to a set of numbers. And my understanding is that they're all one-time codes which are used once, and if they were used again, that it would be possible to crack it.

JM: Right. So it's a shifting algorithm.

Abel: Yes.

JM: Okay.

Abel: So what my understanding of what happened back at the ashram was that something went wrong with the number station. I don't know....

Rupert: It was your parents who screwed up the code probably.

Abel: That's very possible. I've often confronted them with that.

Rupert: Which is why we're all still hesitant to talk to Abel, some of us, but I'll keep it that way.

Abel: But as I explained to you all, I was just a kid then, and I really... I couldn't have done anything. I mean, my parents — and I hate to talk about this, so I won't — they might have had something to do with it. Sloppiness, I don't know.

Rupert: Smoking pot.

Abel: And everybody was then. That was something everybody did.

Rupert: Speak for yourself.

JM: Okay, well, let me move on to another subject, then. The people that... supposedly, in the Amshram story, there are people that have actually migrated to another dimension....

Rupert: The story.

JM: And that there's another ashram in an alternative dimension, on another earth, much like this earth although when it was first found it was unpopulated by human beings. And they have set up a kind of a counterculture organization or disorganization over there, and they haven't come back. Is that true? Has anybody come back? Has anybody tried to contact you from the other side? Once they go, are they gone?

Rupert: Well, to put it out on the floor, I mean now that – I'll say it once more – the Egg's hatched – yes, there are some meetings. We do a special kind of meditation for which we use mediums. And we do try to communicate with this other side that you speak of. As to the real terminology as to what we do during that, I'm not going to really reveal because it's going to be looked upon. I mean, I know there's other members of the ashram that's going to be listening to this somehow, one way or another, because we all keep track of each other. But yes. We'll say that we do try to communicate with other entities. I'll leave it at that.

Abel: Now, my experience with this is that most of what Mr. Bigsby says is true and right as far as I can remember. But part of the communication — the number station, getting back to that — it was communicating on other frequencies. It wasn't just short-wave. And my understanding was that at the time, they were already communicating with people on the other side, partially using that. And these were people that had gone before, like before the ashram even developed. It was, you know, it seems to be something which was handed down at some point in time, the information.

JM: Okay, so there's maybe a connection to the Java2 so-called "lemur beings" that have been encountered?

Abel: It's very possible and very, very likely. I mean, I heard stories, you know, the same thing, when I was a kid living there. We heard stories from old people about moth men back in the day, and the New Jersey devil, the weird creatures that they would see. So it seems, you know, if you connect the dots, it looks like it's....

JM: So there's possibly some sort of pre-existing vortex there? Is that what you're saying?

Abel: I don't know much about vortexes, you know. That's not my field, like I said. But there's something.

Rupert: Like ley lines you know? Something very, very strange.

Abel: Something maybe went wrong a long time ago, and they were just sort of reconstructing to get back to that point. But something, way before the military attack, something had gone wrong. You could just kind of sense it. And it might be wrong as in, you know, a disaster and millions of people dead, but something was just not right. I don't know, like you're in a house when somebody didn't close the door properly and you feel a draft, but you're just not sure where it's coming from.

JM: Okay.

Abel: I think the attack — and I know this is part of the reason that I'm sort of ostracized from most of the rest of the survivors – I think the attack had to do with the communications and the short-wave transmissions. I think the government had people.... I think they'd done this on their own. They had people in other worlds, and I think they were picking up our signals, originating from Ong's Hat, and I think that's what the attack was about. I honestly think they didn't even know that we had an Egg – or Eggs, as it may have been at the time – and they were coming for the transmissions, to stop them, to see who was doing it. And I think they really stumbled upon the Eggs. It just accelerated the situation. I think they didn't... they weren't... they didn't seem to be looking for the Eggs. They went right for the tower, if

I remember right.

JM: Yeah, possibly, that could be. Or I could surmise that they were trying to take the tower out first so you couldn't broadcast any kind of SOS.

Abel: Well, yeah, that makes good military sense.

JM: Sorry. I have a bit of a military mind, anyway.

Rupert: Mixed frequencies and all that aside, I mean, what happens during these meditations, I might add, is just quite a phenomenon. I mean, it really is... these Eggs.... I will mention this: I set aside my, you know, my hesitancy before. I have seen a couple of these devices.

Abel: The Egg.

Rupert: The Egg, yeah. Laying around at certain times in very... like on altars, in the ashram. At specific times they would be there, and then they would be gone when we would expect to see them again. As kids, of course, when we see objects like these, we, you know, were not reluctant to pick them up. We're going to pick them up right away.

JM: So they're actually small enough that you could handle them? They weren't something you climbed inside?

Rupert: Well, no. These... let me get to that.

Abel: Are you talking about the Meditation Eggs, or about the Traveling Eggs?

Rupert: I'm talking about... let me get there. I'm talking about the actual Eggs, which were originally, supposedly, in theory, supposed to be the keys to the bigger ones.

JM: Oh! This is news. Great. Okay. So a smaller egg was a key to a bigger one.

Rupert: That's right. That's what they told us. Now, as to whether we could touch them or not was a different story. No, we couldn't touch them, but we wanted to. I mean, we saw them when they were on altars. We didn't actually... now, that's one of the discrepancies with, you know, with this whole theory is that....

Abel: Which theory?

Rupert: Is the Eggs.... Which Eggs are we talking about? Are we talking about the keys to the actual bigger ones or are we talking about....

Abel: See, we called the keys the Meditation Eggs. That was just my....

JM: Well, see, that's news. To date, in the documentation, there's been no mention of those, so you guys are actually breaking news here that there was such a thing.

Abel: Yeah. I didn't know nobody knew.

JM: No, not publicly. I mean, you have to realize that, I know you guys talk among yourselves, but you're pretty clandestine and pretty tight-lipped and hard to find and a little bit paranoid, I might say – and I don't mean that in an offensive manner; you probably are well justified in your paranoia. But, yeah it's not public knowledge.

Rupert: I did not know this.

JM: Well I don't think you're giving anything away that's going to hurt you or the projects, if there are any more projects going on, but it's interesting from a historical perspective that this is a new development.

Abel: Okay.

JM: So maybe just briefly explain – and we are running out of time – but maybe just briefly explain the unlocking process. I mean, just kind of briefly describe the surface, or what it looked like....

Rupert: They were these small, Easter egg kind of looking devices.

Abel: But they were bigger than, like, a chicken....

Rupert: That's right, they were about chicken-sized.

Abel: No, they were a little bigger. They were bigger.

JM: Like maybe duck-sized, or goose-sized?

Abel: Yeah, like, like, you know....

JM: Ostrich-sized?

Abel: No, no, not that big.

JM: Not that big

Abel: I mean, an adult could hold one in his hand and it was kind of a good size.

JM: Okay, so somewhere between a chicken egg and an ostrich egg.

Rupert: Yeah, they were usually decorated like lingams on altars, like phallic objects that the Hindus worship, and they were usually placed accordingly. There used to be a little clicky device on the left-hand side, just one little clicking device is what it looked like. And the small key access, I should say, were usually different colors.

Abel: Meditation Eggs.

Rupert: Meditation Eggs.

Abel: We used to say. I don't know about you.

Rupert: Well, they're just eggs. I mean, you know, the technical terms for eggs aren't going to go straight here....

Abel: We were talking about them. We knew we weren't talking about the big eggs, the Travel Eggs.

Rupert: Right.

Abel: Yeah. I mean, there were a lot more... I don't know how many Travel Eggs there were....

Rupert: I never actually saw a real Traveling Egg. Let me say that.

Abel: Wow. Okay, yeah. I saw... I definitely saw at least one. I saw what could have been others. Either they didn't look the same; they... I don't know, they looked, like, older or something. I didn't know if they were finished or if they'd ever worked or if they were spare parts, but I know of one that was supposedly the main one. But key eggs – the Meditation Eggs – there were a lot more of them. They were around, you know. People seemed to have them, you know, have them in their homes like I said.

Rupert: Right. Like I said, they looked like decorative, Faberge objects, you know like the Hindus worshipped or something.

Abel: Yeah, they were certainly more like... obviously, not everybody had their own Egg, but, you know a lot of families had – probably most had – at least one of these.

JM: Okay. Let me ask you this one more question and then we'll wrap it up and if you guys want to make a statement I'm going to give you a platform to do that. But briefly, do you feel like you're still under surveillance, that you have reason to hide from the government or some other organizations? Is that why you don't have a singular, organized project anymore?

Rupert: Well, we still talk to each other. I wouldn't say it's not organized, unorganized. I mean, there still is somewhat of a, you know, somewhat of a loop of us from the Hat. And I can't speak for him over there, but we still keep in touch, and what we do, well, trying to reestablish what's going on. I mean, as far as the government's concerned, everyone should keep their eyes open, and no one should... everyone should be suspicious, always. Don't ever trust everything 100 percent. Everybody's possible at... any thing at any time. So....

Abel: I agree. Like I said, I'm not as in touch as Mr. Bigsby is with most of the people because we were a bit more separate from them. And that's sort of still what I do for most of my money today is still helping to run a number station in not only the shortwave kind, but with the CB radio, the CB band which is hardly used now, and even looking into Internet number stations if wireless ever comes into play. So I don't really have too much fear. They could have killed me a long time ago if that was really their intention. And, you know, after the first couple times I talked about it with a few people and they didn't come and kill me then, either, I figured that, you know, I probably didn't know enough for it to be worth them killing me over. But the other thing, by doing the work I'm doing in getting out the numbers, you know, I don't know who I'm working for. I don't know who the money comes from when it's in my bank account. But I just follow the job, follow the orders, and do it and get paid and make a living and I feel as long as I do that, they won't kill me. Why would they? So I'm not that paranoid. I just do what they say.

Rupert: Well, as far as I'm concerned, we have had instances where we were interrogated by a government.

Abel: Recently, or this was after the attack?

Rupert: Well, this was recently, recently meaning after the attack, yes. I mean there's a couple that....

Abel: A ways after the attack, right. Yeah, I heard that they were....

Rupert: They were questioning more of us who, you know, obviously because of the ashram, you know, established itself again as an actual congregation place at one point over on the west coast. And a few of us who started attending there, well, we believed that whoever tipped off the guards in the first place, whether it be frequencies, signals, what have you, military intelligence who's on the inside still, that we're still talking to.... We got debriefed again, but this time it was just the American government, and it wasn't these strange minutemen from Russia, or what have you.

Abel: You could tell they were normal American military?

Rupert: Right. And, you know, a couple of times... you know, and they asked us all the same questions, and it was all based on our history, you know, what we... you know, I mean really ridiculous things. I mean, what we liked to eat, how much money we made. I mean, I guess they were really trying to test if we were foreign bodies or something.

Abel: Yeah, yeah. They never... after the attack, and after we were in, you know, that other town with the safe houses you went over, after that they never really came to us again because, like I said, we just continued where we'd left off by doing the numbers, except we were doing it for them now. And I think that, you know, I don't know. We just did what we were told and everything's been okay ever since for the most part.

Rupert: Well, I haven't talked to Abel since my last visit with the feds, but it looks like they asked him the same questions, too, you know, which gives me reason to believe that all of us are suspect. It's not... I mean, obviously it looks like whatever they're pawning off between us is obviously somebody on their end. So whatever hesitancies and suspicions we have are starting to get.... We're getting closer to the truth. Let's put it that way.

JM: At this time I'm going to wrap it up, but would you guys – either one – like to make a closing statement about who you are, what you want, what you're trying to say?

Rupert: Well, I'd like the US Government to leave us alone. That's one of my requests. We have nothing to hide. We were just kids in an ashram. What can I say?

Abel: Well, I don't have much to say. Just, you know, I didn't know much about the Egg. That's not our involvement at Ong's Hat. I don't know. Maybe they'd leave you alone if you had reason to be left alone. Did you ever think of that? Mr. Bigsby?

Rupert: Well, yeah. Yeah, I can say that we're not really alone, still. That's for sure. But, I mean, as far as ever being left alone, yeah, I'd like to. I'd like to be left alone. I'd like to see that life can be lived to its fullest in peace. And whatever information is out there should be shared by everybody. That goes for whether it's tangible or intangible.

Abel: Yeah, yeah.

Rupert: It should be shared. And anything that you want to know, anything that Denmark wants to know, so be it. I would let them know. We're not hiding out. America's not hiding out. I think the former Soviet Union isn't hiding out anymore, or holding out, and we should just be able to share with everybody.

Abel: Have you... Mr. Bigsby, I know we talked a little bit earlier today, you know, when we were deciding whether or not to do this together....

Rupert: Right.

Abel: Have you thought any more about possibly getting Joe here or letting him see one of the two remaining key eggs or Meditation Eggs?

Rupert: We will, and I think....

Rupert: I've come to the conclusion that maybe we should actually have him take a picture of it for....

JM: Yeah. I was going to ask. That was the first thing on my mind.

Abel: Because, I mean, me and Mr. Bigsby have talked about this several times before, you know, before today, before bringing it up, you know. I thought you knew about them. I didn't know you didn't know about them, but I knew that you hadn't seen one. We were debating whether to let you do that or not, but I think if Mr. Bigsby feels comfortable about it, then I do, too.

Rupert: Excellent. That's fine, that's fine. I feel a little better talking about.... You know, I must say that when it comes to talking about Ong's Hat, it's not always easy, but once you break the ice, we're willing to let you know what you want to know.

JM: Okay, well I look forward to more correspondence and communication with you guys, and hopefully we can get something on film and out to the world.

Rupert: Excellent.

Abel: Fine.

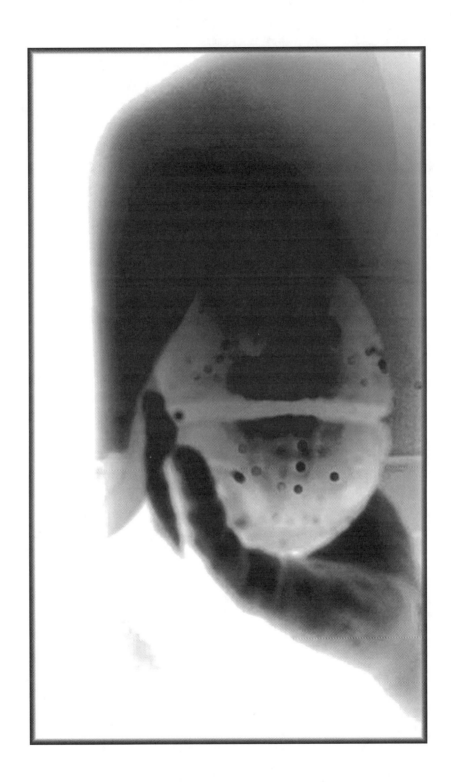

Meditation or Key Eggs: Notes

The images

As promised, Rupert and Abel delivered a "meditation" or "key" Egg for me to examine. I shot a full 24 exposure roll of 35mm film on a Cannon camera and the two pictures below are the only ones that came out. The rest of the roll was "splochy" consisting of large black areas peppered with white "burn" spots throughout. These two pictures would have been about center roll (12 in from the ends). At first I thought the error was due to the camera, maybe a light leak in the body, so I took it in and had it examined at my local professional equipment dealer. It passed all tests and since then I have shot 4 rolls of the same of film, same batch, with no problems. I have been struggling with the negatives to see if I could salvage ANYTHING other than these two very poor quality shots, but it seems that this is all that I can salvage and the best image quality I can get.

Images and their quality

I started with a largely unworkable piece of film, mostly dark and flared, and then I scanned the best photo positive output from that film, tweaked the light and contrast levels on the resultant scan to make it viewable on a CRT monitor, then reduced it to a lower resolution file format (JPG) to make it web servable, which included reducing the color palette so it's browser safe, etc. That explains the striations in the lens flares and weird color balances in the images (notice my neck in photo 1 looks as if it's "covered in blood", as one viewer has noted). Hopefully, next time (if there is a next time), I will be given more advance notice (I was called without warning and told "meet us at xxxxx, now, right now...") so I can better prepare and I will be allowed to bring more than one camera. This meeting had conditions on it, and "only one camera", "no video cameras", and "no pictures of us" (the survivors) was part of the deal. Due to the timing of the call, none of the digital cameras that I have in my studio were readily accessible (I was 30 minutes from the studio at the time of the call). I would have preferred shooting it with my Canon XL1 or at least the GL1, but those are mini-dv (digital video) I am quite aware that a digital camera would have been preferable, but as it turned out, all I had readily available was a Canon EOS ELAN 7E and a Minolta MAXXUM 7. I chose the Canon because it was already loaded with a roll of Kodak Gold Max film.

Photo Log

Photo 1: Shot with the camera on a tripod with a timer, no flash.

Photo 2: Abel's hand holding the Egg.

The Egg : *Taken from my hand written notes of that day.*

    The "meditation" or "key" eggs, as described in the interview with the survivors, were supposedly used to open the larger, "travel eggs". Neither 'survivor' seemed to know how it worked. I felt as if two future primitives were showing me a television remote control and explaining to me what they think it is/was without having ever operated or seen an actual television itself.

I am alone...
More alone in the
Universe than I
have ever been before...
in any memorable point
in time, more alone...

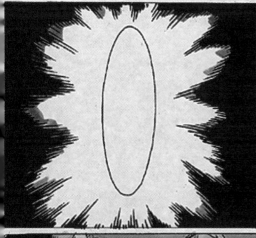

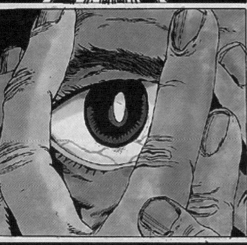

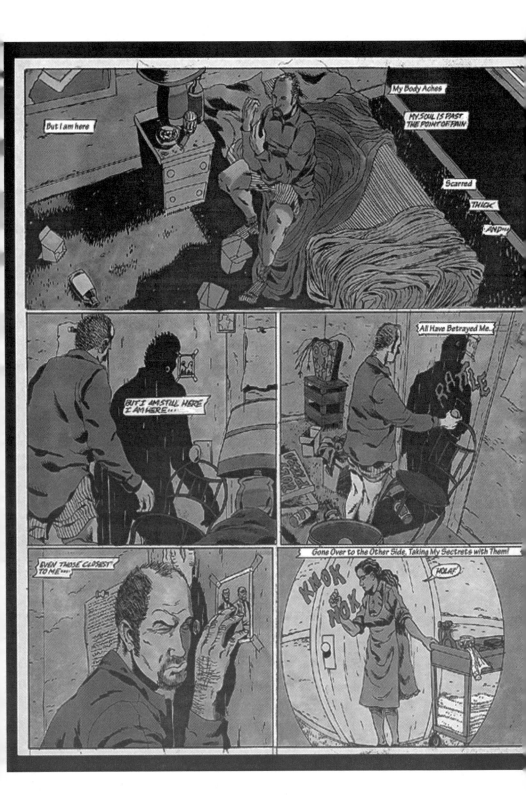

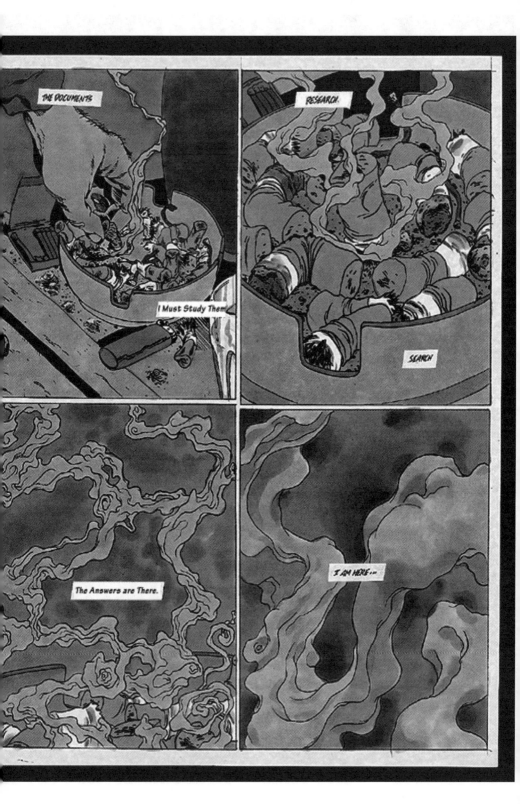

161

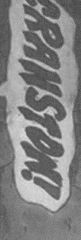

164

165

To be continued

INCUNABULA

INCUNABULA

CHAOS NEVER DIED

Introduction

Epilogue
by Peter Moon

As publication of this material comes to fruition, events and circumstances are constantly changing. It has been a very hard road to even arrive at this point. A primary focal point of literature published by Sky Books is to enable people to look at things they have never looked at before and to increase their understanding of such matters. This includes both scientific and spiritual issues. The idea is to make the collective conscious aware of various aspects of existence that have been ignored, unknown, or hitherto suppressed. This could be called a wave of communication that seeks to inform and enlighten. When such a wave projects itself upon the consciousness of the population, it communicates to whoever will receive it and is repeated and expanded according to the relative merits of the message and the comprehension by the recipients.

There is also something called a counter-wave. Certain ideas that are progressive or that create dynamic change in the culture are often met with opposition or suppression. Gallileo, Joan of Arc, Gandhi, and a host of others have suffered from counter-waves that were induced by an opposition which sought to destroy the ideas propagated by such individuals. The proliferation of ideas concerning Ong's Hat, the Incunabula, and the Montauk Project have all been met with a considerable counter-wave. My entire association with Joseph Matheny has been subject to such. Preston Nichols and I have both suffered from this phenomena since our first book was published. It is rather remarkable that an incredible amount of energy has gone into producing long-winded websites that seek to destroy, suppress, or encumber the proliferation of any ideas concerning the above mentioned subjects as stated in books by any of the above persons. While we well realize that this is a backhanded compliment that indicates our ideas are significant enough to be checked, it should be pointed out that some of these websites and writings indicate that a small army of people have been employed in some fashion to denigrate such information.

The fact that such sites are heavily trafficked indicates that a considerable amount of energy has gone into disseminating them and getting them into search engines. The stories of Ong's Hat and the Montauk Project raise many questions and issues about the way people think. Both platforms indicate that the general state of your average human being does not have a clue as to how the world has been constructed and how he or she might fit into it. Those of you who see the counter-consciousness illusions of society can appreciate what I am saying here. You have already found your way to this book and to the rather unprecedented methods of investigation that are employed herein. That is why the phrase "You have been searching for us without knowing it..." is so applicable to the Ong's Hat saga. If you are interested in this material and learning more about it, you are part of the solution.

The Incunabula and Ong's Hat are a great mystery. From a different perspective than the Montauk Project saga, they allude and sometimes point directly to truths that demonstrate there is a body of scientific information which, if accessed and understood, will raise the consciousness of individuals to where they can reach well beyond the constructs of ordinary human consciousness. The description of the books and literature in the Incunabula catalog are designed to raise people's expectations but, more importantly, their curiosity and interest to such matters. Ideally, it will make one ask questions they had not thought of before and make them think, grow, and expand. The documents were not handed out on a platter although they provide a springboard for those seeking further knowledge. Everyone is encouraged to carry out their own investigations of such matters.

Joe and I have realized that we are playing different roles. I seem to be more of an educator and he seems to be more of a project manager. Joe wants people to ask all the questions they can muster on these subjects so that they can get the entire "Aha!" process going and he can have peers in helping him to resolve the issues at hand. He realizes that maybe 2% of the people who read this book might help him in this regard. On the other hand, I am more interested in laying out a path of clear understanding. This propagates the wave referred to earlier and makes it more possible for that 2% to increase to a larger percent.

We also have to be careful not to define ourselves in fixed roles because, in different aspects, Joe can be the educator and I can be the project manager. I have found Joe to be one of the most education oriented persons that I have ever known. He is very generous about distributing information. Where I come in as a project manager is also interesting, but it seems to be a very low key and background role. I am not even completely aware of it myself. This can best be explained through my association with Dr. David Anderson, the founder of the Time Travel Research Center and the Time Travel Research Association. Although I have known David for several years, he has never appeared in any publications from Sky Books until now. He has appeared in various issues of the *Montauk Pulse* as the President and Founder of the Time Travel Research Center. Until recently (2002), this was a fully active laboratory on Long Island that could actually manipulate time.

The genesis of the Time Travel Research Center began when David Anderson was in the Air Force and had an opportunity to apply his expert mathematical skills to various problems in the defense and satellite industry. Working as a physicist and participating in the advanced scientific research and development programs at the prestigious Air Force Flight Test Center, Dr. Anderson formulated his own breakthrough concepts in the areas of space-time physics and time-warped fields. Upon his discharge from the Air Force, David patented certain patterns of repeating algorithms that are useful in correcting the displacement of satellites which drift several meters away from their previous orbit every year. This is quite a problem to the communications and defense industry and his services and product are in high demand. By patenting algorithms, David was able to create a very lucrative business in the security industry.

Time travel enters the equation because in order to correct the satellite problem, David realized that the most effective way to accomplish this was through time warp theory. In other words, the space-time field of the satellites was actually being manipulated. He was utilizing pure math but also the work of Einstein and many others. While the problem was very unique, David's solution was even more so. In fact, it was brilliant and rather unprecedented in the field of human endeavor.

Of course, if one can manipulate the time-space field of anything, the research is not going to stop there. Having secured contracts with the defense industry, David had a lot of credibility. Investors came aboard to bolster his efforts. Further research established a contained field about the size of a soccer ball which could slow down or speed up time. In other words, if you put in a kitten, it could live a minute for every year you lived or vice versa. Although investors were interested, David never allowed experimentation on animals. The primary use for such a technology is in the medical field where a heart or organ could be placed and preserved indefinitely until such time that a host for the organ could be found.

One might wonder why David came to me. Both he and Preston have a wealth of technical information about such subjects that I will never possess. David explained that the more deeply he probed into physics and the mechanical conditions of space-time, the more he and other colleagues realized that the spiritual function is part of the equation but is largely misunderstood. He felt that he had a lot of catching up to do and was interested in my experience with Scientology and the like.

Although I never saw him very often, David was a very helpful person and graciously hosted the Sky Books website on his Time Travel Research website. Although Sky Books has a new website, you will no longer find any listings on the Time Travel Research Center as it was shut down

The Time Travel Research Center was located on Long Island, but it had to keep switching locations due to severe harassment. David's internet server was also attacked and infiltrated at the same time that Joe Matheny was suffering a similar problem with his. When you get too powerful, the counter-wave theory comes into play. After the harassment, the Government came to David and told him that if he became partners with them, they would take care of his security problems. Forced into a partnership, David was later forced to sever his involvement in the Time Travel Research Center and move away from Long Island. One of the ways they persuaded him was to threaten to hurt people he cared about. He is now working in private industry as an employee. As far as time travel is concerned, David is pretty much a nonperson and his memory has been all but obliterated from the world wide web.

In November of 2001, David called me to his home and explained that he would be going to Russia on a mission for the Government and that he had funny feelings about it. He told me that if he did not return by December 1st that he wanted someone to know about it. David did not return when expected. As soon as I called everyone and made noise to hell and back, I suddenly received an email from David that was sent from Pakistan. He let me and a few other contacts know that he was ok. After returning in January, he was yanked back into the military and was forced out of the time travel business. At this particular meeting with me, he wanted to plan a big event to explain time travel in complete scientific terms and include some of the leading names in academic physics who he knows personally. He also wanted Preston and the other characters from the Sky Books legacy to be on hand. It was not to happen.

At my November meeting with him, David also mentioned that one of the main problems he had in making further advances with his time travel research was that he was not an expert in instrumentation. Well, guess who is one of the foremost experts in instrumentation in the world? Preston Nichols. David and I talked about that and hoped that something could be worked out in the future. This is where I come in as a Project Manager. If I could link up the mathematical and physics genius of David Anderson with the electromagnetic and instrumentation genius of Preston Nichols (who also excels in math and physics as well as a host of other subjects), it would unleash a very powerful team. Throw in the esoteric and computer genius of Joe Matheny, and the consciousness wave is going to be very strong. What a team! Unfortunately, David and Preston are on the "watch list" to make sure they do not get too powerful or proactive with time travel research. Joe and I have not been pressured directly by government figures although we have suffered plenty of counter-wave.

The counter-wave and Dr. David Anderson come into view again when we consider a very well known website known as "WingMakers." The WingMakers are allegedly a group from the future who are seeking to raise our consciousness through a time capsule placed in a canyon near Chaco, New Mexico. Initially I never paid any attention to this website as several friends I know had very good reason to believe that it was loaded with fakery and disinformation. This came to a head in my mind when a prominent lecturer on the UFO circuit aligned himself with the WingMakers website and announced on the discussion board that one of the most secretive, powerful, and dangerous echelons of the secret "government" was called "the Incunabula." Further, he boldly stated that the word "incunabula" means "den of vipers." This was, of course, hysterical to all of us who know that "incunabula" is a Latin word as is defined elsewhere in this book. More importantly, this reveals a counter-wave emanating from the UFO community as well as it infiltrating the WingMakers website. If you look at the WingMaker site, it does not hide the fact that it is connected to the Department of Defense and other government agencies, many of which are unknown. One has to suspect disinformation as a possible ingredient. Whether it is disinformation or not, one has to wonder if there is an actual true story behind it, especially when we consider an excerpt from an interview between Joe Matheny and Emory Cranston (pg. 122 of this book). Some have said that WingMakers is an off-shoot project that is delivering on the following promise made in 1993 (pre-WingMakers). The excerpt is as follows:

JM: Who were the occupants of Java2 , that left behind the ruins?

EC: Well, that's the biggest news of all really. We found them — or rather they've found us. They claim to be an alternative evolutionary branch of Homo Sapiens through h.Javanesis and h.Neanderthalensis. They look like they're descended from lemurs rather than chimps, like us. A bit like the characters from Javanese shadow puppet plays. They discovered how to travel long ago, in a time we might think of as the time of Atlantis or Mu (only we would be wrong...) It's all rather Lovecraftian, in as much as they claim to be responsible for certain aspects of human culture, aspects which are uncanny, but not maleficent. Not only in Java. The Tuatha de Danaan of Ireland who vanished "underground ", and other "faery" and "hollow earth" clues...the whole idea of another physical world, not a heaven or hell, but a Magickal universe next door...anyway, we were wrong about them. Traveling in time, either fast forward or backward. They simply set out to explore the Series. They think it may be endless, and some decided to return "home" to Java2. They're a completely non-hierarchic segmentary society, like primitive hunter/gatherers, but with a highly evolved culture. A lot of Terrans have completely "converted" to their way of life, even their language. You should hear their music! The returnees brought back some of their artifacts and...well, "furniture" I guess you'd call it. Their ancestors built a city during a "High Civilization" period in their history, but they rejected hard technology for cognitive sciences long ago. Our travel techniques are crude by comparison and lacking their whole mythopoetic value system. We're planning soon to release certain archival material here in Earth Prime, certain bits of art and music, which we expect to act in a viral fashion to produce profound paradigm shifts. The traveller's culture is now, I believe, our most effective *"weapon"*.

When I finally looked into some of these matters, I started by looking in *The Time Travel Handbook* by David Childress. The chapter on WingMakers is divulged by a mysterious "Dr. Anderson," a man who worked for some of the most secretive government agencies imaginable. "Dr. Anderson" is the one who identifies the WingMakers as a mysterious group from the future who deposited a time capsule in New Mexico. As I read the chapter, I was surprised to notice many synchronicities between "Dr. Anderson" and Dr. David Anderson. Some of these were of a personal nature and concerned things I knew about him from direct conversations that others would not know about. So, there is a definitely a case to be made for these two people being one and the same. There is also a case to made against them being one and the same. The primary argument for them not being the same is that David does not talk about the future, aliens, and secret government projects. If this were David, it would have to be a part of him that is "compartmentalized." We do know, however, that David is very secretive and that both Dr. Andersons are experts in security. While "Dr. Anderson" claims to have security systems which lock out the CIA and KGB, David Anderson, until recently at least, made a healthy share of his living in the security business. "Dr. Anderson" also indicates that he defected from the government projects because they had implant technology that could wipe out his memory. While we cannot say or even imply that anyone's memory has been wiped out, it is obvious logic that anyone involved in such matters would be very careful about what they say to whom.

Another telling aspect about the Anderson connection is that "Dr. Anderson" claimed that he aimed to take the technology he learned to the mainstream. It should be noted that David Anderson was doing exactly that until he was recently curtailed in his endeavors. David had broadly publicized his Time Travel Research Center and lectured at the University of Miami and other such institutions. Confronted by scoffing and arrogant physics professors and students, he would routinely win them over by pointing out things in common science that are routinely overlooked. He was even planning to write a text book that would lay many matters to rest for good. David knows his stuff. Unfortunately, Dr. David Anderson is lost to us for the time being although he indicated to me there might be some sort of comeback in the future. The WingMakers website has since deleted the name of "Dr. Anderson." Although I have queried them on this point, I have yet to get any response.

In such an environment, secrecy and security become the primary and most important subjects that need to be studied. Time travel projects like the Montauk Project and Philadelphia Experiment are immersed in secrecy. Up to this time, too little is known about them. Therefore, if one cannot blow open the holes of secrecy by studying the security leaks and fragmented data that is available, one has to tackle the subject of "secrecy" itself.

The secrecy obsession even extends to Brookhaven Labs. At a public lecture in 2001, Preston Nichols and myself listened to one of the top academic physicists in the world explain how information can literally be encrypted within the structure of atoms. For those familiar with Brookhaven Lab's legendary role with the Montauk Project and time travel, it is more than ironic that they would have also developed a subject which could be termed "atomic security." I am not talking about protecting nuclear weapon secrets either. "Atomic security" refers to utilizing atoms in a secretive nature. More importantly, the term itself blatantly alludes to the idea that the mystery of the atom itself can be decoded. If the human genome can be decoded, why not the atom itself? Actually, this idea is not new to science. They have been working on it for centuries. The approaches to decoding the atom have not worked. If anyone has gotten close to decoding it, they have been whisked away by secret forces and thus you have never heard of them. Secrecy is a cult. The secret societies you hear or read about are the cult. "Real knowledge" is booby trapped with many systems in place that are designed to restrict us from huge data bases of information.

There is also a very humorous irony involved in a white-coated PhD decoding the very structure of the atom. When he does so, in the fullest and truest sense, there will no longer be any need for scientists. The mystery is completely gone and there is nothing left to study. The atom is currently recognized as the basic unit of creation. If you can penetrate its secrets, you can literally mold and manipulate matter in a way that has previously been reserved only for God, the Jinn, or other supernatural beings. Basic logic implies that God or these supernatural beings are therefore part of the aforementioned secrecy cult. Do we have a mess on our hands or what? No one has to be a specialist in understanding human character to understand that any scientist discovering such powers would be tempted to use the power thus discovered to manipulate other beings for his own aggrandizement or benefit. And, if the powers over creation that we often call God are benevolent, why have they not clued us in on the mystery? Perhaps this is why our adversary in these matters has been called El Diablo, or the Devil. "El Diablo" means "the double" in Spanish, but it also derives from the root word for "dios" or God.

In the above tradition, it may interest you to know that the most influential, if not the greatest, scientist of the last millennium was also the world's best cryptographer and is the founder of modern cryptology. Believe it or not, he was known as "007" — the same name Ian Fleming used for James Bond. He collected the largest library of alchemical, hermetic and occult texts the world had known since the destruction of the Library of Alexandria. His name was Dr. John Dee, and he was the court astrologer of Queen Elizabeth I. The tradition he embodied had been around for a long time. Much of it had come to him via the remnants of the Knights Templar tradition. Most of the texts he collected were in an encrypted format. The nature of the atom and the powers of creation that influenced it had been part of occult tradition for millennia. It was in this legacy of scholarship that Dr. Dee studied the nature of angelic beings and their counterpart: demons. They represented the forces of creation that reigned behind the material illusion we know as atoms, a word that phonetically approximates Adam, the first man, but also represents "*at-om*" where *om* represents the sum of creation through the sound of *om*. If we consider that om originated from the word *ong* (as described in the forward to this book), an atom could have been called "*at ong*" as in Ong's Hat.

The more you study the universe and the matters referred to above, you will understand that the universe itself is a mysterious encryption system. Not only is matter encrypted, but so are the faculties of creation that erected it. People get so sheepishly excited when media shows try to make one tremble over questions such as "Who created the pyramids or some such ancient structure?" The answer is simple. It's the same bastards who run the media and have you watching a dumb show that tweaks your mystery button but whose whole reason for being there is to sell you a Fortune 500 product. It is the priest class versus the working or slave class. At least watching television while you eat Fortune 500 cereal is better than being conscripted to build a pyramid as a slave in ancient Egypt. For the most part, the passage of time has improved the lot of the common man. As for television, people would be better served by watching Bart Simpson do a school report on "Who in the hell invented the atom?"

Both Aleister Crowley and Jack Parsons pursued John Dee's work in their own magical workings. They not only recognized the encrypted nature of the universe, but their genetic pool is intimately tied to the forces and faculties of creation referred to above. Still, both looked to Dr. Dee for leadership. Dee encapsulated a summary of his scientific and magical knowledge in a work called the *MONAS HIEROGLYPHICA* or *HIEROGLYPHIC MONAD*. It could be said that if one wanted to bring about a total enlightenment of humanity that this could be accomplished by deencrypting this monad. The word association with MON, the first syllable in "Montauk" and the name for the "hidden god" as in A-MON is not coincidental. The decryption of the entire universe is at hand. A considerable amount of work has been accomplished already. We plan to share it with you in a subsequent book: *Synchronicity and the Seventh Seal: The Search for Ong's Hat.*

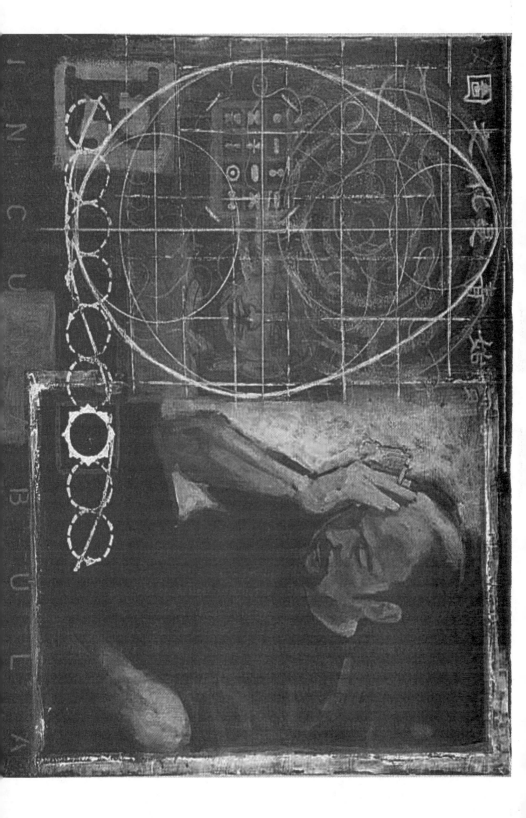

Afterward
by Joseph Matheny

Many people have asked me over the years what I think this all is. So, I'm going to give you what I think in a nutshell. Peter Moon and I will flesh it out much more in the upcoming book, *Synchronicity and the Seventh Seal: The Search for Ong's Hat.*

Now to the nutshell. Or should I say *Eggshell*? What I think the *Incunabula* represents is an entrainment module for Quantum thinking. It is packed full of memes and concepts that do not yield up singular answers but rather lead to a form of Quantum logic that supercedes singular answers and the *need* for singular answers. There is no secret plan for building an Egg and the Egg as a physical travel device may not even be the point. However, the Egg *as a symbol* is all-important. I'm going to do the unthinkable here and refer you to a book. It is available for free on the Internet with a little hunting. That book is John Dee's *MONAS HIEROGLYPHICA* also called *THE HIEROGLYPHIC MONAD*. Find it, read it, and if you're lucky you can also dig up Diane DiPrima's thoughts and works on it as well.

I personally believe that humanity in its present form is not ready or capable of travel to other dimensions nor do I think we'd be welcome by several species that are. We still carry too much baggage as a whole. I have come to this conclusion after three intense years of experimentation in the media to divine the percentages. I do however suspect that the next stage of evolution of consciousness on this planet will be capable, ready, willing, able, and welcome in the multiverse.

Looking back through the Akashic records of this planet and planetary system, one can clearly see that humankind is not the first nor will it be the last experiment in Gaia node consciousness. One only has to look around with clear and honest eyes to see that this present form (humankind) has clearly plateaued and has been skidding across the plateau for some time now. As is the rule with this described state, what sets in is *entropy*.

I say, disentangle yourself from the last traps, namely those of nostalgic romanticism and fear, and get on with the next step, or as my friend Denny so succinctly put it, "Bring it". Whether you or I personally want it to happen is of no consequence anyway now, is it? Why not be a facilitator rather than an agitator? Why not surf the wave rather than have it wash over you?

Humankind only holds the potential for immortality. It's not guaranteed. The information stream encrypted within the *Incunabula* is not for everyone and the laws of evolution would seem to support that. The first appearance of a mutational curve in a species represents 2% of the total population. Through attrition, the 2% which have mutated to be more adaptable to the changing environment eventually become the 100% and then another 2% pops up, ad infinitum.

Evolution= Change= Chaos

If you're not sure what I mean by Chaos, study the nature of Chaos in fractals and the work of Ralph Abraham, especially his book *Chaos, Gaia, Eros: A Chaos Pioneer Uncovers the Three Great Streams of History*. Then, come back to that formula and I think you will see that I am not espousing riots in the streets (although that may be a symptom of the change) but rather a return to the primal matrix of creation, the Qabbalistic 0, the Formless Ocean.

It would seem that our mission as agents of change is to prepare ourselves, our particular consciousness node, for the neXt step. Pave the way like a modern day John the Baptist or an Avatar. Should you accept this mission, be aware that it is a long, hard and lonely road to travel, since you are one of 2% and that is a low percentage. However, you can go to sleep each night knowing that you are facilitating the arousal of the new form, and looking around, you may have moments of clarity and say to yourself, "It's about time."

Good luck. Will I see you "over there"?

QVI NON INTELLIGIT, AVT TACEAT, AVT DISCAT.

MONAS HIEROGLYPHICA
IOANNIS DEE, LONDINENSIS,
AD
MAXIMILIANVM, DEI GRATIA
ROMANORVM, BOHEMIÆ ET HVNGARIÆ
REGEM SAPIENTISSIMVM.

IGNIS

AËR

DE RORE CAELI, ET PINGVEDINE TERRAE, DET TIBI DEVS. Genes.

Guliel.Silvius Typog.Regius, Excud. Antuerpiæ. 1564.

Synchronicity & the Seventh Seal:
The Search for Ong's Hat
by Peter Moon

In his most ambitious work to date, Peter Moon summates and synthesizes his own experiences with synchronicity and accelerates this process to an unparalleled level as he reveals his deepest occult mysteries yet.

In the early 1990's, as was reported in Montauk Revisited, Amado Crowley boldly announced that he would reveal the secret behind the murder of Aleister Crowley on the 50th anniversary of the magician's death. December 1, 1997 came and passed with nothing but silence. Critics of Amado hailed this as "proof" that he was a charlatan. Prior to this, Amado and Peter Moon had indulged in a lengthy and intriguing correspondence which was suddenly and mysteriously terminated when Peter discovered the truth. Amado blamed the interference between him and Peter on the Solar Temple Lodge, a cult which received broad media recognition with ritual "suicide" deaths in France and Quebec.

Peter sat on this secret for years and only shared it with three people (including Cameron before her death) before he met Joseph Matheny, the primary facilitator of the Ong's Hat legend. This secret served as an occult bonding agent between Joe and Peter in their very first conversation and has served as a catalyst in their collaboration on releasing the material on Ong's Hat and what is now being called the unveiling of the Seventh Seal.

Besides the intriguing occult legacy of the Wilson-Crowley connection, this work explores the real life Emory Cranston, a genuine character who stands on the edge of parallel realities. His interactions with Joseph Matheny are expounded upon as well as his mysterious connections to the Moorish Orthodox Church. Delving deeply into the quantum paradox of Hassan Sabbah, the legendary leader of the Assassin Cult, the deepest secrets of the Islamic mystery schools are revealed.

The most highlighted and adventurous aspect of this new work is the tracing of the magical residuals of Crowley and Jack Parsons back to John Dee and his Incunabula catalog, a document which helped inspire the Metamachine©, a device designed to generate synchronicity and to literally "hack our way into heaven."

Can it be done?

With or without you and I, scientists and engineers are already well on their way to utilizing organic computer chips. Organic matter has DNA. If you are communicating with computer chips, this means that you can ultimately communicate with DNA via a computer. DNA can be programmed and manipulated as never before. The implications of this research are astounding and can literally link thought to matter.

Synchronicity and the Seventh Seal: The Search for Ong's Hat will expand your viewpoint to unprecedented horizons. The genie's bottle has been uncorked. You are invited to make the link.

The Montauk Pulse™
A CHRONICLE OF TIME

A newsletter by the name of *The Montauk Pulse* went into print in the winter of 1993 to chronicle the events and discoveries regarding the ongoing investigation of time travel and related subjects. Originally designed to focus on the Montauk Project as reported on by Preston Nichols and Peter Moon, it has remained in print and been issued quarterly ever since. With a minimum of six pages and a distinct identity of its own, *The Pulse* will often comment on details and history that do not necessarily find their way into books.

Through 2002, The *Montauk Pulse* has included exciting new breakthroughs on the Montauk story and will now include updates on the Ong's Hat phenomena, material related to this book, and the further research of Joe Matheny as it can be shared.

Subscribing to *The Pulse* directly contributes to the efforts of the authors in writing more books and chronicling the effort to understand time and all of its components. Past support has been crucial to our continued existence. We appreciate your support in helping to unravel various mysteries of Earth-based and non-Earth-based consciousness. It makes a difference.

■

For a complimentary listing of
special interdimensional books and videos —
send one dollar to:
Sky Books, Box 769, Westbury, NY 11590-0104

SkyBooks

We wait for ALL checks to clear before shipping, including Priority Mail orders. If you want to speed delivery time, use a U.S. Money Order or credit card. Those orders will be shipped right away. Complete this order form and send with payment or credit card information to: Sky Books, Box 769, Westbury, New York 11590-0104

Name	☐ This is my first order
Address	☐ I have ordered before
City	☐ This is a new address

State / Country	Zip

Daytime Phone (In case we have a question) (   )

Method of Payment: ☐ Visa ☐ MasterCard ☐ Discover ☐ Amex ☐ Money Order ☐ Check

—   —   —   Expiration Date

Signature   Date:

Title	Qty	Price
The Montauk Pulse (1 year subscription).....................$15.00		
The Montauk Pulse back issues (List at bottom of page.) $3.00 each		
List:		
Subtotal		
For delivery in NY add 8.5% tax		
Shipping: see chart on the next page		
U.S. only: Priority Mail		
Total		

Thank you for your order. We appreciate your business. Contact us by email at skybooks@yahoo.com

United States Shipping — Allow 30 days for delivery. For U.S.only: Priority Mail—add the following to the regular shipping charge: $4.00 for first item, $1.50 for each additional item.

Under $30.00 ....add $4.00
$30.01 — 60.00 ...add $5.00
$60.00 — $100.00 add $7.00
$100.01 and over ..add $9.00

International Shipping Rates for SURFACE SHIPPING ONLY. Due to the vastly different costs for each country,we will not ship by air. Only credit cards or checks drawn on a U.S. bank in U.S. funds will be accepted.

Under $30.00.........add $10.00
$30.01 — $50.00..add $15.00
$50.01—$ 75.00 ..add $20.00
$75.01—$100.00 .add $25.00
100.01 and over...add $35.00